CRIME MOST FOUL

When a teenager attacks an old lady, her best friend, Detective Constable Sheldon, wants revenge. Chief Superintendent Bill Hallam of North Central Regional C.I.D. forbids Brenda Sheldon to get involved in the case. Ignoring the ban her investigation, aided by Dave Morgan, leads her to a drug racket in Deniston. The trail is obscure until Molly Bilton tries to help a man involved with the drug pushers, but finds the man murdered, and her own life in danger.

GEORGE DOUGLAS

◆

CRIME MOST FOUL

Complete and Unabridged

LINFORD
Leicester

First published in Great Britain
by Robert Hale Limited
London

First Linford Edition
published 2006
by arrangement with
Robert Hale Limited
London

British Library CIP Data

Douglas, George
  Crime most foul.—Large print ed.—
Linford mystery library
  1. Policewomen—England—Fiction
  2. Murder—Investigation—England—Fiction
  3. Detective and mystery stories
  4. Large type books
  I. Title
  823.9'14 [F]

ISBN 1–84617–416–3

Published by
F. A. Thorpe (Publishing)
Anstey, Leicestershire

Set by Words & Graphics Ltd.
Anstey, Leicestershire
Printed and bound in Great Britain by
T. J. International Ltd., Padstow, Cornwall

This book is printed on acid-free paper

1

Just before six o'clock on an evening in late October, a youth was cycling along the street in the Deniston suburb of Heathfield. He darted anxious glances to left and right as he approached the small general shop set on a corner. There seemed to be nobody about, but the shop's one window was still brightly lit, as if there might be some business yet to be done that day.

Dismounting, he propped his cycle upright against the high kerb and stepped across the pavement to peer through the glass door. Satisfied that there was nobody in the shop, he took a last quick look around, then pulled a nylon stocking mask from a pocket and forced it over his thick brown hair, his narrow, large-nosed face. He pushed the shop door open, and as its bell clanged, closed it firmly behind him.

A small, white-haired woman with a

1

cheerful rosy face came bustling through from the living quarters.

'Eh, you're only just in time,' she began. 'Another minute and I'd have closed. Oh!' Her eyes had focused on the masked face.

The youth produced a small glass bottle and removed its stopper. He spoke in a high voice, brittle with nervousness.

'This is strong acid, missus. Now you wouldn't like it all over your face and in your eyes, would you? So just open that till and give — quick!'

The old lady swallowed hard. 'Nay, don't be daft, lad,' she said. 'You can't get away with that, you know. Me husband's in the kitchen — Hey, Jack, come here — ' She raised her voice quaveringly.

The youth laughed harshly. 'Stop kidding, missus. You haven't got a husband. You haven't even got a dog. There's just you and me here, so . . . ' He leaned across the counter and the bottle in his right hand moved threateningly towards her.

She grabbed at his fingers, twisting

them, forcing the bottle mouth away from her. Liquid splashed over the evening paper which lay on the counter. Still gripping his fingers tightly, she looked down. The paper was unharmed. She said, 'That's not acid, you — ' and then he lunged forward, striking at her with his left fist.

The blow was clumsy enough, but it smashed into the shopkeeper's face. She jerked backwards like a puppet, her head hit the edge of a shelf behind her and she slid, crumpling up on the floor without even a moan. The youth uttered a sharp, panic-laden cry of dismay. He shoved the small bottle into his pocket, clawed off his nylon mask and fumbled his way out of the shop. He turned his cycle, sprang on it and pedalled away, head down, his knees pumping like supercharged pistons.

Fifty yards away, from the opposite direction, an elderly man was walking towards the shop, with an Alsatian dog on a lead. He marked the youth's hurried exit and disappearance and his brows drew together in sudden concern. Quickening his pace, he reached the shop, looked through the open door, then stepped inside.

'Mrs Avery! Hullo!' he called.

There was no reply, but the dog strained forward on its leash, its hackles rising. The man called again, 'You all right, Mrs Avery?' and the Alsatian, whining now, heaved itself up to rest its front paws on the counter. The whine ended in a short, angry bark and the man, leaning over his dog, saw the motionless body and swore, a harsh expletive in which rage and shock were mingled. Then, with a command to the dog to sit, he banged up the counter flap and dropped on his knees beside the sacklike figure. In the slack wrist he seized he felt a faint beat.

He sprang up, stepped over the woman and reached for the telephone standing on a shelf by the rear door. His fingers were trembling, but he controlled them with an effort as he dialled.

★　★　★

It was a matter of routine at Kingsmead House, headquarters of the North Central Regional C.I.D., that serious crimes throughout the area should be reported there by teleprinter from the various police divisions. Thus, Detective-Inspector Robert Joynton, of Deniston East Division, forwarded, on a Tuesday morning, details of the attack on Mrs Gertrude Avery, investigated by his staff the previous evening.

Chief Superintendent Bill Hallam, head of Regional, duly saw the report, noted that Joynton did not request assistance, and gave a few moments of his busy day to reflecting what he would do to young thugs who beat up defenceless old ladies, even when the said thugs came from broken homes, which happened, so the theorists claimed, in around ninety per cent of such cases. Hallam, versed in the practical side of his job, knew differently.

He was dealing with the rest of the morning's reports when a tap sounded on his office door. He called a cheery, 'Come in!' and smiled a welcome to his visitor.

Woman Detective-Constable Brenda Sheldon was tall and slim. Chestnut hair crowned an attractive, faultlessly-modelled face, but today her deep grey eyes, usually alight with the vivacity of youth, were set in a stern coldness and there was no answering smile on her lips as she came into the room. Hallam saw the tenseness of her movements.

'There's something the matter, isn't there, Brenda?'

She thrust forward the copy of the local paper she was carrying.

'There's a report here, sir, of an attack on a shopkeeper in Heathfield. An elderly lady named Gertrude Avery.'

Hallam nodded. 'I haven't seen the Chronicle this morning, but I've an item here from East Division. Inspector Joynton's case.'

'Mrs Avery is a life-long friend of my mother, sir. In fact, she's always been Auntie Gert to me.'

'Brenda! I'm most dreadfully sorry!' Concern showed immediately on Hallam's lean face. 'Is she . . . ?'

'She's alive, sir, but only just, it seems.

We rang St Margaret's this morning. They say her condition is still serious.'

Hallam gestured at a chair. 'Sit down, and let me see what the Chronicle says about it.'

He scanned the few lines quickly and put the paper down with a grunt of disgust.

'Same old story!' The words came savagely. 'Fellow got clean away! Your friend was lucky in that this man Baker, with his dog, caught a glimpse of the chap and had sense enough to investigate. Otherwise . . . ' He paused. 'They don't normally use push-bikes,' he said thoughtfully.

'A neighbour happened to know Mrs Avery was a friend of ours, sir. She telephoned mother, who went along to the shop at once. We live only a stonesthrow away. But the police were in charge by then, there was nothing she could do.'

'Mrs Avery is a widow?'

'Yes, sir. Her husband died some five years ago, she's continued to keep the shop running.' The words came stiffly from Brenda's taut lips.

'You're upset about this,' Hallam said sympathetically. 'And that, of course, is perfectly natural. But she'll have the best of care and treatment at St Margaret's, you know. It's a case of hoping for the best. And if there's any question of visiting her in hospital, just do so, at any time. There'll be no need to ask permission to go off duty for that.'

'Thank you, sir. You're very good. But there's something else.' She hesitated, then went on quickly. 'I'd appreciate it very much if you'd put me on this case. I'm more or less free just now, and — '

'Just a moment,' Hallam cut in. 'I'm afraid that's impossible. Inspector Joynton hasn't asked for assistance, and you know we can't go butting into a divisional job until we're requested to do so.'

The girl's face showed her disappointment, but not her acceptance of Hallam's ruling.

'As I said, sir, my home is in Heathfield. I know the locality and many of the people who live there. Especially those who are Mrs Avery's neighbours.

And, before I was transferred here, I worked for a time at Orville Street Station, Mr Joynton's headquarters. I thought, if he were reminded of this, he might possibly agree to let me come in to assist.'

''Might possibly',' Hallam repeated. 'You don't sound too certain about it, do you?'

For the first time Brenda showed signs of nervousness. Hallam had the impression she wasn't sure if she should proceed further. Then she took a deep breath.

'You know Mr Joynton, of course, sir?'

'Fairly well. I wouldn't say we were intimate.'

'I know him very well, sir. And I know exactly how he's going to treat this case. He'll work thoroughly, very thoroughly, on it for a day or two and then, if he doesn't get results, he'll drop it.'

Hallam replied with a touch of reprimand in his voice. 'You have been in this game long enough, Brenda, to know that in these attack jobs, if a lead doesn't turn up in twenty-four hours, the chances are it never will. And no division is so

9

well-staffed, nor so idle, to have men running around in useless circles merely for the look of the thing.'

'I realize that, sir, and I thought if I, with the special knowledge of the district I have — '

Hallam cut in on her again. 'You had better realize also, that as far as I am concerned, the subject is closed.'

Brenda bit her lips, swung to her feet. 'Very good, sir. I'm sorry if I've said too much.' She drew herself up very stiffly. 'I have ten days leave owing to me, sir. You said I could take it when we weren't particularly busy here. May I have permission to go on leave as from today?'

Hallam looked at her from beneath half-lowered eyelids. For several moments he considered her carefully, then he said,

'Sit down again, Brenda.' And when she had done so, he went on, 'You're personally involved in this attack on Mrs Avery, of course. I understand how you feel. You want, above all things, to find the culprit and bring him to justice. You think you could be more successful in this than Inspector Joynton and his men.' He held up a hand as she was about to speak. 'Let me finish. Suppose I believed you that such would be the case. Suppose, also, that Inspector Joynton asked for our assistance. You would be the last person on my staff I'd send along to help him. And you know why, don't you?'

She nodded glumly. 'You've told us, sir, that when a police officer becomes emotionally involved in a case, he or she can't assess evidence accurately, can't be sure of taking the right steps, since a police officer must never work with a personal bias.'

Hallam allowed himself a grin. 'I'm glad my staff lectures aren't all a waste of time. Seriously, though, I appreciate your problem. I'd feel the same, in your shoes. But nothing can be done about it. The attack on your friend has given you a severe shock, naturally. You'll adjust to that, and if I know you as well as I think I do, you'll adjust very quickly. And that, I think, is about all.'

Again Brenda stood up, facing him resolutely.

'Not quite, sir. There's the matter of my leave.'

'And if I grant it to you, I need only one guess how you propose to spend it. Correct?'

'I have certain plans, sir.'

'And I, as your superior officer, have power to forbid you to carry out those plans.'

The colour left the girl's face. 'With the utmost respect, sir, I disagree. On leave, I can please myself what I do.'

Hallam took out his tobacco pouch, reached for the pipe in his ashtray, tapped it out, began to reload it slowly.

'Miss Sheldon,' he said, 'I took a certain amount of trouble to have you transferred here to Regional. I did so because I decided you were the type of woman officer I needed on my staff. Until this moment, I've had no cause to regret that decision. But now I find you on the edge of insubordination.'

Impulsively, she flung out her hands. 'It's not that, sir, really! It's just — ' Her arms fell to her sides. 'You know what it is,' she said in a voice which was almost a whisper.

'So, in your desire for personal vengeance you are prepared to risk dismissal from Kingsmead House?'

She raised her head to look squarely at him. He saw the sudden decision in her eyes.

'No, sir, not that. I — er — Please, could you forget all I've said? I'm willing to drop the whole idea I had — now.'

Hallam set a match to his pipe, puffed blue smoke. Through it, Brenda saw the twinkle in his eyes and she let go a long breath of relief.

'I don't think that's possible — to forget what you've said, Brenda.' He flicked the dead match into the ashtray. 'Your leave is granted, as from now. And you can do what you like with it. But listen carefully. If I get any sort of complaint at all that you're interfering in any way with Mr Joynton's business, you'll be back in uniform before you know where you are. You understand?'

'Oh, I do, sir! And thank you very much. I — ' She struggled for words which wouldn't come, she only managed another 'Thank you, sir,' before she turned to the door. Hallam's voice came again as her fingers reached for the doorknob.

'And, unofficially, Brenda, the very best of luck! Whatever happens to Mrs Avery, I hope with all my heart you'll get that thug!'

2

Brenda went back to the main office, where Detective-Sergeant Garrett, busy with a pile of forms, glanced up at her.

'Well, any luck about the leave?' he asked.

'Granted as from now.' Brenda crossed to her own desk. 'I — er — I explained the circumstances to him.'

'You mean about your mother's decision to run the old lady's shop while she's in hospital? And that you'll be helping her?'

'Something of the sort,' Brenda prevaricated. She began to clear up her desk, her hands moving deftly. Garrett pushed his papers aside, leaned back in his chair.

'I've often thought I'd like to keep a little general shop, you know. Dishing out packets of cigarettes and weighing up sweets for the local kids. Though they tell me standing behind a counter tends to give you varicose veins. You watch that,

Brenda. It would be a pity to spoil — ' He broke off, noting her frown of irritation. 'Sorry, love. I should have realized you're not in a mood for light chit-chat today.'

'That's all right, Dick.' She locked her desk, put the keys in her handbag. 'Be seeing you, then.'

Garrett nodded. 'Have as good a leave as possible.'

She said 'Thanks,' and went down to the car park, unlocked her car and drove slowly away. Her talk with Hallam had put a shadow of doubt in her mind, had weakened her resolution temporarily. Was she being too much carried away by her desire for personal revenge? Wouldn't it be better . . . ? She shrugged the thought away as she turned into the main road and quickened her speed.

She drove homewards by way of Heathfield High Street, where Mrs Avery's shop was situated. As she got out of her car opposite the shop, a lanky, ginger-haired, cheerful-looking young man came out of the doorway. His grey-green eyes widened.

'Brenda! Light of my life! So, without a

word to his faithful henchman — me, as if you didn't know — the old man has called in Regional, eh? And Regional has sent its glamour girl!'

Brenda knew Detective-Sergeant Swayne very well and liked what she knew. But now she looked at him unsmilingly.

'Cut it out, Sarge. Mrs Avery is my mother's best friend, and mine. Is mother here? She said she would be.'

Swayne's face had set in lines of deep concern. 'Gee, I'm sorry, Brenda. I simply didn't realize . . . Yes, your mother is here though I didn't know she was your mother. I mean, she told me her name, but not having met her before I didn't connect her with you.' He paused. 'I'm twittering on like this because I'm so damned sorry I started chi-hiking you, when you must be . . . '

'That's all right, Sarge. Tell me, how's it going?'

The carroty head was shaken mournfully. 'It's about gone, I'm afraid, as far as we're concerned. In fact, I've just told your mother she can turn that 'Closed' sign on the door to 'Open'. She says she wants to keep the shop going. Honestly, we've tried everything and we haven't the ghost of a lead. The only bright spot about the whole business is that I've just rung the hospital again — we've a W.P.C. on bedside duty there — and they now think there's a fair chance the old lady will be all right.'

'I'm certainly glad to hear that!' The shadows swept from Brenda's face. 'You're going back to your H.Q., then?'

He nodded. 'We'll keep enquiries going on this, of course. But — Well, the fact is, we're madly busy, and . . . '

'I know.' Brenda gave him a wave of farewell as she moved towards the shop and he got into his car.

She found her mother inside, dusting off the counter. Mrs Sheldon, tall like her daughter, but with darker hair and complexion, looked up with a warm smile.

'Brenda! We've just heard from St Margaret's — '

'I know, mum. Sergeant Swayne told me. Isn't it great?'

'It's made my day, dear. And so you've

got your leave granted? That means we shall be able to run this place between us. I'd better show you the system Gertrude uses, then you can take over when I have to slip home to see to things there.'

Brenda leaned on the counter. 'Listen, mum. I asked Mr Hallam this morning if he could put me on this case. But there's no hope of that. So I'm going to work on it unofficially.'

Her mother's dark brows drew together. 'No need to tell you I'd give everything I have to see that fellow brought to justice. But d'you think you can do more than Inspector Joynton and his men have already done?'

'I'm going to have a try. I'll give myself two days on it and if nothing turns up by then . . . ' She shrugged.

'You won't get yourself into trouble, working on your own?'

'I'll risk that. And, look, I want to get started at once. I'm going across the road to see Mrs Gill.'

'Inspector Joynton has talked to her already, Brenda. He told me so.'

'Then I won't be interfering, having a

chat with her. I shan't be long.'

With swift strides she crossed the road and knocked at the door of a semi-detached house, its front garden ablaze with chrysanthemums. A thin, white-haired man answered her summons, peering at her through thick-lensed spectacles.

'Why, it's Miss Sheldon!' he greeted. 'Eh, that's a bad do about Mrs Avery. And you such friends with her, an' all.'

'We've just heard there's an improvement, Mr Gill. Look, I know you've had the police here, making enquiries.'

'We have that! Not as we could tell 'em anything much. But come in, Miss Sheldon. The missus'll be glad to see you if you can spare a moment.'

Brenda followed him upstairs to a front bedroom where an elderly lady, seated in a chair by the window, smiled warmly at her. Mrs Gill had been crippled by arthritis for many years.

'It's right grand to see you, love,' she said. 'But I'm sorry about Mrs Avery. What a do that was! Have you heard how the poor thing's going on?'

Brenda gave her the latest news, and Mr Gill slipped out to get on with his housework. Brenda waited until the old lady had expressed her opinions on thugs and what she'd do to them if somebody would give her a chance.

'You've had the police here to see you, Mrs Gill?'

'Oh, yes. Somebody told 'em how I sit by me window all day and half the night, watching all that goes on . . . Well, as you know, love, it's me only bit of interest, like.'

'And did you see anything, Mrs Gill?'

'Like I told the fellow that came, detective inspector he was, or so he said, and if ever I've seen a chap with a big opinion of himself . . . However, I said I'd seen this youth ride up, go into the shop and come out again. And this inspector asked me to describe him, which I did as best I could. Late teens, I said, tallish, thin, brown hair, big nose. And he — the inspector — said how could I be so sure, because it was getting dark. As if he thought I was making it up. And he kept calling me 'Ma', which is something I

21

can't abide. He knew my name, why couldn't he use it?'

Brenda refrained from any comment.

'Well, I told him my eyesight was pretty good, and, what's more, I'd seen the same young fellow standing outside the shop once before, some days ago. And he said, was I sure about that, could I swear to it in a court of law or was I only just fancying it because I couldn't really have had a proper look at him last night. And I got a bit mad at that and told him if he didn't believe me, why was he bothering me at all? So then he cleared off, and glad I was to see him go. But now they've sent you to talk to me, Brenda, I'll tell you what I didn't tell him.'

'Actually, Mrs Gill, I'm on leave at present. But anything you know could be very helpful.'

'Right. Well, I'm pretty sure that young chap was around here — let's see — last Friday afternoon, it would be. I saw him come on this bike and he stood for a long time, looking at the shop window, then he went in and came out with a packet of something in his hand. And just as he did so, who should come tripping along but that young Karen Harkness, wiggling her bottom and showing her legs up to the tops of the thighs. Legs? I've seen better on an old kitchen chair!'

She paused, and Brenda thought she looked a little uncomfortable.

'You told Mr Joynton you were certain you'd seen him on Friday, Mrs Gill,' she said gently. 'But now you say you're 'pretty sure' it was the same young man.'

'Yes — Well — ' The old lady's knotted fingers twisted together in her lap. 'It could have been the same — I think. But when you get to my age, dear, and suffer quite a bit of pain off and on, you do tend to get a mite confused.'

Brenda smiled at her. 'That doesn't matter a bit. But you were telling me something about a girl. Karen — Harkness — was it?'

'Oh, yes. Well, whether the chap I saw on Friday was the same as done Mrs Avery or not, he and this Karen stood there talking for some minutes. I'm sure about that. But then, that young madam 'ud talk to any fellow. If I was her mother . . . '

Brenda let her ramble on for a while before she took her leave. Downstairs again, she asked Mr Gill where Karen Harkness lived.

'Second house past the garage,' he answered promptly and didn't enquire her reason for the question. He saw her out and Brenda, thirsting for action, walked down the road to knock at the door of the house just past the garage. Her summons was answered by a big woman with heavy features and ash-blonde dyed hair.

Brenda had her warrant card ready. 'Mrs Harkness?' she asked as she thrust it forward. 'We think it's possible your daughter may be able to help us with our enquiries in to the attack on Mrs Avery, at the shop.' And she held her breath, because if Inspector Joynton or one of his men had already interviewed this family, she was certainly putting her foot in it.

But the large lady merely smiled genially. 'I'm sure Karen would be glad to help you, though I don't see how she can.

She was at home all last night. However, she isn't at work today, so come right in.' She stepped aside and called, 'Karen! Somebody from the police to see you!' She added to Brenda, as she showed the visitor into a neatly-furnished lounge, 'Karen's on holiday just now. She works at the Public Library.' She drew out a chair. 'You won't want me, I suppose? I've some baking in the oven.'

Brenda said that would be all right and as Mrs Harkness went out, her daughter came in. She was a slender, pretty girl with dark hair and hazel eyes. Seventeen, Brenda judged. Karen wore jeans and a shapeless cardigan. Both garments were spotted with paste and paint.

'I'm sorry I'm in such a mess,' she apologized. Her voice was low-pitched, attractive. 'But I'm in the middle of decorating my bedroom, you see.'

Brenda smiled. 'And, of course, I've called at just the wrong time. You have a piece of wallpaper half-pasted, or you're just in the middle of a particularly tricky bit of painting?'

The girl laughed. 'Neither, actually. I

was longing for an excuse to take a break. Mum says you're from the police?'

Brenda still had her warrant card in her hand. She passed it over. Karen read it solemnly and handed it back.

'Looks genuine enough to me,' she said, and grinned impishly. 'Of course, in these days, you can't really tell, can you?'

'So you'll have to take a chance.' Brenda found herself liking this girl. Maybe, as old Mrs Gill had alleged, she was fond of the boys. So what? She seemed the type who knew how to take care of herself.

'I'm here,' Brenda went on, 'because there's a chance you may be able to help in this wretched business at the shop last night. Now, I know you were at home then — your mother has told me so — but it's possible you talked last Friday afternoon with the man who attacked Mrs Avery. You did have some conversation then, outside the shop, with a young fellow?'

Karen looked thoughtful. 'Friday afternoon — yes, I did. And I'll bet I know who told you. Mrs Gill, the Ever-Seeing

Eye. Ah, well, poor old thing, she doesn't have much fun. Yes, I went to the shop for mum, and there was this boy hanging about outside. He had a bike. He said, 'Hello!' and I said, 'Hi!' and he said, 'D'you live around here, then?' And I said, 'Who wants to know?' All that sort of thing. And then we sort of chatted on from there.'

'You can describe him, I'm sure?'

'Let's see — he'd be eighteen or nineteen, tall, thinnish. I can't tell you what colour hair he had — it wasn't fair, I do know, because I rather go for fair boys and I'd have noticed . . . Oh, yes, I remember he had a big, beaky nose and a birthmark, about the size of a ten new pence coin, on the angle of his jaw, right hand side of his face. He seemed a bit sensitive about this, I thought, because he kept it turned away from me most of the time.'

'Did you notice the make of his bike?'

The girl shook her dusky head. 'Sorry. I'm not interested in bikes unless they have engines.' She grinned engagingly again.

Brenda looked up from the notebook she had taken from her bag.

'You've given a good description, anyway. What did you talk about?'

'He did most of the talking.' Her eyes widened and she stared at Brenda. 'D'you know, come to think of it, he asked me a lot of questions about the shop — who owned it, did the shopkeeper live alone, did she keep a dog for company. Makes you think, doesn't it, now Mrs Avery has been set upon? And like a twit, I gave him the right answers, I never thought, you see.'

'Don't worry about that, Miss Harkness. You weren't to know what he had in mind — if it really was the same fellow who went into the shop last night. What else did he ask you?'

'Nothing more about Mrs Avery. He started to get more personal, like, and wanted to know about me. Did I live in Heathfield, what did I do with my time — that sort of thing — you know — like when a boy's working up to ask you for a date.'

'Did he actually do that?'

'No, not really. Anyway, if he had it in mind, he'd have been unlucky. I didn't like him. There was something about his eyes. And he seemed right jumpy all the time, as if he wanted to be off and yet couldn't make the effort. I got properly fed up with him eventually and said I'd have to be going. Which I did — into the shop. He called after me if I ever went to The Groove to keep an eye out for him, because he sometimes went there. And that was all.'

'The Groove,' Brenda repeated. 'That's the cafe in Lambert Street?'

Karen nodded. 'It reckons to be a right swinging spot. I don't know much about it — never been in there. I'm not very keen on such places, I suppose you could call me a bit of a cube, really.'

'And none the worse for it.' Brenda got to her feet. 'Thank you very much, Miss Harkness. I won't take up any more of your decorating time.'

'Have I been at all helpful?' The question came eagerly.

'You may have. It's a line which certainly will have to be followed up.

Thank you again.'

Karen said, 'Any time,' and showed her out. Brenda walked slowly back to the shop. Because D. I. Joynton had got off on the wrong foot with Mrs Gill, and so hadn't been told of Karen's conversation with the youth with the bicycle, she herself had picked up a possible lead which the official enquiry had missed. And now what? It was her own duty to hand this information on to the proper quarters. And yet ... There was no definite proof that the youth who had spoken to Karen was the same who had attacked Mrs Avery. Until this was established — and possibly it never would be — the enquiry could go no further than it already had done. Knowing Joynton, and putting herself in his place, Brenda was certain — or she persuaded herself she was certain — that he wouldn't be inclined to waste more time on it. Therefore, it was definitely up to her to step in here.

Having made up her mind, she rejoined her mother in the shop. Mrs Sheldon was already busy with customers, most of whom wanted to stop and discuss the business of the previous evening. On her mother's suggestion, Brenda readily agreed to go on home and have lunch ready for the shop's midday closing hour.

Brenda spent the afternoon as a shop assistant and quite enjoyed the new experience. But when they had closed for the day and she had had an evening meal, she announced she was going into town and might be late back. She got her car out and drove towards the city.

Lambert Street, where The Groove was situated, lay behind the Deniston Civic Centre. The cafe was garishly-lit and was sandwiched between a furniture store and an employment agency. At a quarter to nine on this mild October night the cafe juke box was filling the street with noise, but since it wasn't a residential area there weren't likely to be any objectors, Brenda thought as she parked her car at the kerb.

She walked along the pavement, glancing into the cafe as she passed it. Practically all the customers were youthful — she had expected that. Several of them, of both sexes, were sitting alone at the small tables, apparently waiting either for dates to turn up or hoping that another lonely soul would suggest a pairing. It seemed an orderly, well-run place, presided over by a stout, bald man who stood behind the counter in a white jacket over his bulging trousers. A tall thin young man with long hair and square-framed spectacles was moving around with a trolley, collecting empties.

Brenda turned and went through the open door. The stridency of canned music inside was almost deafening, and the groups who made up most of the customers, having drawn several of the tables together, had to shout in order to make themselves heard, despite their nearness to each other. Brenda wove her way to the counter and received a cool stare from the fat man before he turned away to fill her order for white coffee.

'You ain't one of our reg'lars, I think,' he said as he set the cup down and took her money. Brenda raised her eyebrows.

'Do you have to be some sort of a club member to come in here, then?'

A wheezy chuckle answered her. 'O' course not, luv. I'm glad to see you, and I hope you'll come again.'

Brenda smiled. 'That depends on the taste of this coffee.'

'So we'll be seeing you again for sure,' he returned smartly.

Brenda took her drink to an empty table against one wall, halfway down the room. She hadn't liked the calculating look the fat man had bestowed upon her when she had gone to the counter. It hadn't been exactly welcoming, and she wondered why. She was absolutely certain she had never come across him in the course of her work and she couldn't believe she had been recognised as a plainclothes policewoman. She shrugged, she was possibly letting her imagination run away with her.

Stirring her coffee, she looked carefully around the room, but there was no youth present whose description matched that which Karen Harkness had given her.

The coffee was certainly good. As she lowered her cup after a tasting sip, her attention was caught by a couple at the next table, both teenagers, a youth and a girl. They were sitting there without talking, and there was an air of almost painful tenseness about them.

The bespectacled assistant approached their table. Watching covertly, Brenda saw him give a quick, meaningful nod to the young man before passing on. The youth got up and made his way towards the counter. He turned to the right before he reached it, and with a quick glance around as if to make sure he was unobserved, he ducked through a curtain which hung at one corner of the room, alongside the counter.

And at that moment half-a-dozen youths came swarming in from the street and Brenda at once smelt trouble.

3

Yet the newcomers hadn't the look of a gang of hooligans, out to do a place over for kicks. There was an air of definite purpose about them as they surged up the room towards the counter, talking and laughing together. They gave the impression of a disciplined body of young men under orders rather than of a mob held together only by a loose, undefined urge to make mischief.

Brenda glanced at the stout proprietor, saw he had stiffened into an attitude of wary suspicion as he eyed them. His assistant, too, had stopped his trolley-pushing and was staring, his head thrust forward. But few of the customers seemed disturbed, though Brenda noticed the newcomers were receiving admiring glances from some of the girls.

On the whole, these lads were worth looking at. They moved well, like athletes in training, there were no long-haired weeds among them, though their clothes and shoes were modernly-styled. They lined up at the counter and gave their orders civilly enough, coffees and cokes in about equal proportions. They waited at the counter until the proprietor, panting a little in his efforts to deal with this rush of custom, had served the last of them. Then one of the youths, a tall, fair-haired lad with a humorous quirk to his mouth, gave a nod, like a leader issuing an order. Five of the six turned and marched down the room, their drinks in their hands, looking for vacant seats. The remaining youth, slim, dark, rather on the small size in height, went directly to an empty place near the curtain through which the lad from the table next to Brenda had gone. Brenda saw the proprietor, still watching them, blow out his fat lips in what was clearly a sigh of relief and his assistant began to trundle his loaded trolley towards the service hatch at one side of the counter.

The fair-haired youth, about to set his coffee cup down on a table, and with his back to the advancing trolley, seemed to sway to his rear. One edge of the trolley caught him beneath a hip, he stumbled forward and his cup and saucer went flying from his hand to smash on the floor in a stream of liquid. At that moment the juke box moaned into temporary silence.

'You clot!' There was a look of fury on the tall lad's face as he swung round upon the assistant. 'You did that on purpose! What goes, then? You looking for trouble?' His voice rasped startlingly loud in the sudden quiet.

The assistant, for all his greasy hair and short-sighted eyes, wasn't going to take that one lying down.

'Use your loaf, mate,' he returned reasonably. 'You stepped right back without looking. It was an accident, let's leave it at that.' And he bent to retrieve the fallen crockery. As he did so, one of the tall youth's companions, a thickset, barrel-chested redhead, gave him a violent shove. The assistant fell forward on his hands and knees, and some of the customers, not liking the look of things, got up hurriedly and made for the door.

The fat man crashed a huge fist on his

counter. 'That's enough of that, now!' he shouted hoarsely. 'You lot drink up and get out of here — quick! and I don't want to see any of you around this place again!'

'Really, dad?' The blonde leader grinned mirthlessly at him. 'And suppose we like this joint, grotty as it is, and decide we'll stop on a bit? We might even rough it up a little while we're here.'

'Look, young man.' Wrath darkened the fleshy face. 'You try anything more on, and I'll have the police here so quick you won't know if it's Christmas Day or your Aunt Kate's birthday!'

'Coppers? Huh!' The youth sneered. 'Think we're scared of that crummy lot? Go on — ring 'em. And we'll be back again sometime, with a crowd of our mates. And that's a solemn promise.'

The proprietor glared but he made no attempt to reach for the telephone on a ledge behind him. By now the situation had become indeed explosive, the remaining customers were obviously prepared to enjoy its outcome, too. The slightest spark, and up would go the rocket.

That spark was provided by a couple of young men in leather jackets who were sharing a table with two similarly-clad 'ton up' girls. The men exchanged glances, got to their feet. One of them, burly, beetle-browed, spoke loudly to his mate.

'Come on, Jim. Let's take these nits. They've asked for it.' And around him other youths, with the light of battle in their eyes, were also rising. The proprietor swung round, grabbed at his telephone.

Brenda, meanwhile, had been sitting drinking her coffee, keeping a general eye on things, but vastly intrigued by one circumstance. Why had the slim dark youth left his friends and gone to the table near the curtain, where he was cut off from the rest of his mates? It didn't make sense to her. Now, as the moment for the free-for all was clearly imminent, she saw the leader look towards that solitary figure and raise his hand in what was obviously a signal. The other nodded, rose quietly and slipped behind the curtain.

There was plenty of movement in the

cafe now, people were milling about, some trying to get near the centre of disturbance, others seeking places where they would be out of the way. The assistant had darted behind the counter, the fat man was dialling, nobody seemed to notice Brenda as she got up from her chair and moved towards the curtain. The girl at the next table had hurried out of the cafe at the outset of the developing trouble.

Brenda reached the curtain, drew it aside. Behind it was a short passage, at the end of this she saw the foot of a flight of uncarpeted stairs. A door which led back into the cafe, behind the service bar, was on her left. On her other side, a blank wall.

She went forward to the stair, looked up to an empty landing. The noise behind her was increasing now, but over it she could distinguish a series of thuds and angry shouts from above her head. The Groove was having quite a lively evening. And it sounded as if somebody on the first floor was taking a beating.

She ran up the stairs, reached the

landing. A door facing her was shut, but another on her left was partly open. Inside was a room which contained a small table and two chairs. On the table were papers, a stack of filing cards and a tray containing money in notes and silver.

The slightly-built lad who had sat by himself was doing his utmost to fend off the attacks of a couple of men, either of whom Brenda wouldn't have been surprised to find in a Rogue's Gallery. The boy was cornered, his mouth was bleeding, but he had his fists up in defence and still seemed full of fight.

One of his assailants, a lean, wiry character with protruding teeth, aimed a kick at the boy's stomach. He saw it coming and turned to avoid it, dropping his guard. The other man promptly piled in a right hook which sent the youngster's head jerking back, puppet-like.

Brenda went into action. As the kicker's foot dropped back, she swung her heavy handbag at his face from behind. He staggered, she dropped the bag and crooked her right arm round his neck, gripping her right wrist firmly with her other other hand and pulling to get him off balance. He brought up his left knee to swing his foot rearwood in a crashing back kick, but Brenda's judo training had taught her to expect the move. She jumped sideways, landed with her feet apart and threw him, using one hip as a fulcrum. It wasn't a very neat throw but it was effective. Her opponent cannoned into a corner of the table and went down gasping.

The other man swung round to see what was happening behind him. The boy whom he was attacking slid, somewhat muzzily, from the corner where he had been trapped. Brenda snatched up her handbag, grabbed the boy by a shoulder and rushed him out of the room, slamming the door behind her.

The tumult in the cafe below had ceased as if every person there had been paralysed into silence. Brenda knew that meant the police had arrived and she didn't want to risk running into anybody who might possibly recognise her. She jerked at the handle of the other landing door, which opened to show a short passage with two closed doors on one side of it and a wall, broken by a grimy window, on the other. Pulling her charge through, she shut the door and, finding a key in the lock on the other side, turned it.

The boy was recovering from the beating up he had received. He nodded as she said, 'Come on,' and began to hurry along the passage. He was just behind her when, at the end of it, they came to a second flight of stairs, leading downwards. These were uncarpeted, they ended in a small concrete-floored hallway, with a closed door to the left, and, behind the stair, a passage leading back from what was clearly the rear door of the premises.

This was locked, and bolted on the inside, but the noise of its opening brought nobody to investigate. The two emerged on to a littered backyard with a door in its surrounding wall. Beyond the door they found an alley which led out to Lambert Street.

Before they reached the main road Brenda stopped and looked at her companion. 'You all right?' she asked.

'I'll live.' He grinned crookedly as he pulled out a handkerchief and mopped at his still-bleeding lips. 'And thanks a lot, miss,' he added. 'You sure do know how to take care of yourself.'

'I thought you weren't doing so badly, either. What's your name?'

Johnny Pitts, miss. I — er — well, it just struck me as a bit odd, like, you turning up when you did.'

'That's quite a story, Johnny. And my name's Brenda. Now we know each other, suppose you give me your side of it first.'

He shook his head. 'Sorry. I can't do that. I'm under orders, sort of, to keep my mouth shut. And, anyway, I think we ought to be moving on out of here.'

'Good idea. We'll talk in Lambert Street. Come on!'

She strode ahead of him, and, reaching the street, saw a two-man patrol car pulling away from the entrance of The Groove. At the same moment Johnny Pitts ducked past her, swung right, and launched himself into a fast sprint, heading past the cafe.

Brenda sighed in annoyance. She wasn't going to chase him, of course. But she was certain he had information which could be of use to her, which would, at least, allay her curiosity. And then, as the flying form passed beneath a street lamp beyond the cafe, a tall figure sprang from the shadows and grabbed his shoulder. Brenda recognised the fair-haired leader of the trouble-making gang. She walked quickly towards the pair.

Johnny was talking in breathless gasps, jerking a thumb over his shoulder in Brenda's direction. The other lad, however, showed no desire to make a getaway. He waited, keeping Johnny by him, until Brenda came up. Then he stepped forward, looking closely at her.

'Hi!' he said coolly. 'Johnny's just been telling me you got him out of a very nasty spot. And, of course, you want to know what it's all about.' He had a pleasantly-deep voice and his accent had none of the uncultured inflexions he had used in the cafe. 'I say,' he added, 'you were in The Groove when the shindig started, weren't you? You were sitting alone at a table by the wall.'

Brenda nodded. 'I was, but I left to follow your friend Johnny. What happened inside after that?'

'Fatso — the proprietor, that is — rang the police. But we'd done what we'd come for by then — at least, I hoped we had. So when the law arrived, things had just about sorted themselves out. There wasn't much done in the way of actual damage — a chair leg broken, two cups smashed — I said I'd pay for them, and did. Upon which Fatso decided not to prefer charges. It's business as usual in there now.'

Johnny spoke up. 'Where's the others, Ted?'

'Gone their separate ways, as arranged.' He turned to Brenda again. 'I was hanging about waiting for Johnny to turn up, you see. I have a car yonder' — he nodded at a Morris 1100 parked across the street — 'so maybe I could drop you somewhere? The least I can do, after what Johnny has told me.'

'Thanks, but I've my own car here.'

Brenda smiled at him. 'As you said a few minutes ago, I want to know what it was all about in there.'

He regarded her solemnly, dry-shaving his chin. 'The whole business is rather awkward,' he said. 'I don't know if I have the right to tell you, Miss — er — ?'

'Sheldon. Brenda Sheldon. And I'm sure you needn't be quite so mysterious.'

He shrugged. 'My name's Ted Blake, I'm known for obvious reason's as 'Sexton' to my pals. Look, I'm keen to hear how you got into the act, too. I wonder . . . There's a phone box across the street. If I could ring my — er — principal — I think we could work something out, if you're really interested and don't mind waiting a few moments?'

'You go ahead,' Brenda agreed. This talk of principals and being under orders had become extremely intriguing. As Blake strode across the street, she turned to Johnny, who was cautiously testing the firmness of his teeth with a thumb and finger.

'Quite a lad, your Master Ted Blake,' she observed.

'Sexton? He's the greatest.' The words came indistinctly. 'Got all the answers, and strips well, too.' He ceased his oral investigations. 'Not too bad. One of 'em's a bit loose but maybe it'll tighten up again. They do, don't they, miss?' he added anxiously.

'Frequently,' Brenda replied. She was watching Ted Blake in the phone box. Clearly, he knew the number he was ringing by heart and he seemed to get through at once.

The conversation he had was somewhat protracted. At Brenda's side, Johnny moved restlessly while she waited with the philosophic patience her training had bred in her. But at last Ted put the receiver down, recrossed the street to join them.

'Sorry about that,' he said. 'It took longer than I bargained for. And now things are more complicated than ever, you being a policewoman, Miss Sheldon. Were you on duty at The Groove tonight?'

Brenda managed to keep her composure. 'I wasn't, as it happens. And I take it you learnt of my profession from whoever you rang just now?'

He nodded. 'From Dave Morgan. Any bells ringing?'

'Morgan,' Brenda repeated thoughtfully. 'Just a minute. There's someone of that name who runs a physical culture place in Duncan Street.'

Ted Blake beamed. 'The very man. And one of the best. When I gave him the main facts just now, and mentioned your name, he asked me to describe you, which I did, and he said he knew who you were, had met you once and would like to meet you again, so, if you'd care to take up the invitation now . . . '

Brenda said, 'Right. I'll get my car.' She turned away and the other two crossed the street to the Morris 1100.

As she got into her own car and drove towards Duncan Street, three-quarters of a mile away, she called to mind the Morgan case, one of the first she had been on after her transfer to C.I.D. Lewis Morgan, eighteen years old, and a weak character if ever she'd seen one, had been rounded up with three other men and charged with shop-breaking. Young

Morgan, having asked for six similar offences to be taken into consideration, had been sent for Borstal training. During the investigation Brenda had met his father, a big, burly man with a tonsured scalp of coal black hair. The elder Morgan was obviously grief-stricken and shocked at the discovery of his son's criminal activities. He had seemed to blame himself for some fault in the upbringing of his boy. Brenda had done what she could to help him with advice and comfort.

And now she was going to see him again, for it must be the same man, surely? She wasn't quite clear why she was on her way to Duncan Street — events had moved so quickly this evening she hadn't had time to line them up. She would have to play the next bit entirely without a script.

It certainly was the same Dave Morgan. He was waiting for her as she drew up behind Ted Blake's Morris. She turned from locking her car and he greeted her, and now the Welsh lilt in his voice was clear of the sorrow which had blurred it at their last meeting.

'Miss Sheldon! Good it is to see you again. And as pretty as ever, too!'

Brenda shook hands with him, almost losing her fingers in his great paw. She looked beyond him where, over a narrow entry between two warehouses, a brightly-painted sign proclaimed 'School of Physical Culture. D Morgan, Prop.' And in smaller letters, 'Entrance far end of court.'

'You look very well yourself, Mr Morgan,' she said.

'Mis-ter Mor-gan,' he repeated, separating the syllables. 'Look, now, it's 'Dave' with everybody.'

'Fair enough.' Ted and Johnny came up to join them and Dave said, 'Well, let's go in,' and turned to lead the way through the court entrance.

At the end of it was a building with double doors and a smaller door lettered 'Office' at the side. 'Used to be a warehouse,' Dave explained. 'I bought it cheap, and with a bit of help from various people, converted it into a gym and general training quarters. Show you

51

round, I will, sometime. We're closed up now, actually.'

He opened the office door and ushered her up a flight of narrow steps to a small landing. The two youths followed them like sheepdogs. Brenda recollected that Dave Morgan had been a professional boxer who had done very well for himself in the ring. On his retirement he had taken over a garage and filling station.

'Is this a full time job with you now?' she asked as he moved past her to open the office door.

'Oh, no. Just evenings and weekends. Still in the motor trade, I am. Only, you see, there isn't a lot of opportunities for lads around here to keep fit and — and all that.' He ended the sentence abruptly and pushed the door wide. Then he said, on a note of surprise,

'Hello, Derek! What you doing here, then? I thought you'd gone home like the other lads, I did.'

Brenda recognized the thickset, ginger-haired youth who had pushed the assistant to his hands and knees at The

Groove when the trouble had started there.

'Thought I'd just hang around, Dave, in case I was wanted.'

'Thanks, boy, but there's no need for that. I got to have a few words with this lady, and I haven't had the griff from Johnny yet, but — well, that's about all.'

'Okay, Dave, just as you say.' He gave them a general, 'Goodnight, all,' and clattered away down the stairs.

The office was small, with a flat-topped desk in the centre, half-a-dozen wooden chairs, shelves which held manuals of physical culture and books on various sports, pieces of apparatus stacked in corners. Dave Morgan moved behind the desk and Ted Blake sprang forward to place a chair for Brenda.

'I'll take Johnny and clean him up while you talk to Miss Sheldon, Dave,' he said, and the pair went through a door at the back of the office. Morgan seated himself, rested his enormous forearms on the desk top and grinned at Brenda.

'Who starts the talking, now?' he asked. 'You? Or me?'

4

Brenda had already made up her mind on that point. Whatever business this was, she wanted to make her own position clear.

'I was at The Groove tonight unofficially,' she said. 'That is, I was there for a personal reason. I want to find out the identity of a young man who sometimes goes there. He wasn't among those present tonight, though.'

Dave Morgan shrugged his massive shoulders. 'Unofficial. Personal reason,' he repeated. 'I don't quite get it, now. I'd have thought, if you wanted to track somebody down, you'd have done it as a policewoman, like. I mean, you'd be in touch with all the set-up necessary, wouldn't you?' And when Brenda didn't reply he went on quickly, 'But you had good cause, no doubt. You still at Orville Street, Miss Sheldon?'

Brenda told him of her promotion to

Regional and Dave's white teeth flashed in congratulation. 'Tell me one more thing,' he said. 'Are your people interested in this Groove cafe for any reason?' He spoke the name of the place as if it were poison in his mouth.

'Not at all, as far as I'm aware. But you are, Dave. That's obvious.'

He nodded. 'I've reason to believe there's quite a bit of drug-pushing goes on there behind the scenes.' His voice was harsh, bitter. 'But maybe I'll know more about that when I've talked to Johnny.' He jerked his head in the direction of the washroom door, then leaned forward to her again, his dark eyebrows drawn together.

'Lewis, my lad,' he said. 'You'll remember him. He's still at that place where the law sent him. Oh, it isn't grumbling I am, he asked for it. Look, now, he got into bad company. And I couldn't think why, because his mother and I did our best . . . But it was easy money he was after, see? More than he got, working for me. He wanted money because he'd started taking drugs. And I didn't know. Daft I must have been, not to see it, you'll say.'

'Not at all,' Brenda responded. 'I've come across other cases where the parents didn't realize what was going on.'

She wondered if Dave had really heard her. He was wanting to get the story off his chest, could hardly wait to pour it out.

'It was when he was sent away that it was discovered, see? The M.O. there spotted the signs that Lewis had been on this stuff. And he got the story out of Lewis, did this doctor, and then he wrote to tell me all about it.'

Brenda sat there, listening to a tale which was becoming all too frighteningly familiar to members of her profession. The desire of a youth to be 'with it' and to boast he was 'on the stuff', an enjoyment of the stimulation brought by the amphetamine-barbiturate compounds, an enjoyment which became a compulsive habit. Then experiments, heroin and LSD, until the subject, whose original wish was merely for kicks, became hooked, an addict, desperately needing his 'fixes,' desperately, too, needing the money to pay his pusher, the drug-peddler.

During the recital Ted and Johnny returned quietly to the room. It was clear they had heard the story before.

'My lad,' Dave went on, 'is having treatment and they say they'll cure him. Got to him in time, see? So he'll be lucky, but what about all the other boys and girls like him? Scares me to think of it. That's the main reason I started this gym stunt here. Thought if I could keep only one from the road Lewis took, it 'ud be worth all the time and trouble.' He relaxed, and looked up and across at the two lads, smiling paternally. 'They're good boys that come here — all of 'em. Look you, talked myself out, I have. I'll let Sexton tell you about tonight.'

Ted Blake drew his chair forward. 'Has Dave told you of our suspicions re The Groove, Miss Sheldon?' At Brenda's nod, he went on, 'Where the information came from doesn't matter. And it didn't seem particularly reliable, at that. However, Dave thought we should follow the said whisper up. Last Saturday night we sent

57

Johnny here along to do a recce, since he's a dim, inconspicuous type.' He neatly avoided the kick Johnny aimed at his ankle. 'Johnny noticed four fellows, all teenage, slide behind that curtain in the corner, one at a time. He thought they looked rather the junky type, he followed one of them out and saw him take a small bottle from his pocket, shake something from it into his hand and swallow whatever it was. That decided us to probe further into the matter — and when I say 'us', I mean we took our orders from Dave.'

'You'll be saying,' Morgan broke in, 'that we should have gone to the police, Miss Sheldon. But, look you, if we had, and they'd accepted the evidence we had for them, which was no real evidence at all, they'd have been a bit . . . Well . . . '

'Heavy-handed about it,' Ted supplied. 'You know, making enquiries first, and all that, could have scared the birds clean off.'

'Actually, we don't work that way,' Brenda replied. 'But do carry on, please.'

'Right. Under my leadership, with

Derek Noyes who was here just now as second in command, we went to The Grove this evening and staged a bit of a diversion to give Johnny a chance to see just what went on behind that curtain. I think we did rather well, too, considering we had to play it off the cuff, don't you?'

'Any rookie policeman could have seen you weren't the real trouble making type as soon as you put your noses through the door.' Brenda said it with a smile. 'Still, for raw amateurs, I suppose you didn't do so badly.'

Ted bowed. 'I shall treasure that piece of warm appreciation all my life. Now it's Johnny's turn to spout.'

'Yes, indeed,' Dave said eagerly. 'I've been waiting for that.'

Johnny cleared his throat. 'Behind the curtain there's some stairs leading to a landing. I stood on this landing and listened. I heard voices in a room on my left. I couldn't hear much because of the row in the caff underneath. But it seemed to me some sort of a deal was going on inside there. Anyway, this door opened and out came a kid about my age. He looked at me and said, 'You're unlucky, mate. Shop's closed for tonight. Something on down below.' And he opened that other door, Miss Sheldon, the one we came through that leads down the back stairs, and he mizzled.'

'Do you remember what he looked like?' Brenda asked. Johnny considered for a few moments.

'Taller'n me, spotty face, George Best hair style.'

Brenda nodded. 'I saw him go through that curtain just before you people came in.'

'Well,' Johnny continued, 'he'd not closed the other door behind him, so I took a quick butcher's through it, and saw one of those two fellows at this desk, packing what looked like little bottles into a briefcase. Couldn't see the other, but he musta spotted me, for all of a sudden the door was jerked wide open and out he rushed and grabbed me.

'I tried to get away, of course, but I couldn't. He dragged me into the room and held me, and both these characters looked at me and the one with the briefcase asked me what the 'ell I thought I was doing there. And before I could answer the other said, 'He's not one of our clients, Chuck. I guess he's just one of those nosy little boys. And he oughta be taught a lesson.' And this Chuck said, 'I couldn't agree more. He's loitering with intent on private property, and that's unlawful.' And he gives me a sorta nasty grin and then they both went for me.' He smiled crookedly. 'I'd have bin a right mess now if Miss Sheldon hadn't turned up.'

'You didn't see any other signs, besides the bottles, to prove that was some sort of a drug-pushing game?'

'Hadn't a chance, miss. They were on to me too quick.'

'I reckon he saw enough, though,' Dave broke in eagerly. 'You're in on the police side of such business, Miss Sheldon, so do we report to them?'

Brenda replied slowly. 'We find the main trouble in such cases is this. You pick up the odd pusher, he gets done for it. But he's only a small unit in what could be, and most likely is, a big and ugly organization.' She made a sudden decision. 'Look, you leave this to me. I'm on vacation at the moment but I'll have a talk to my chief about it over the phone tomorrow morning. I know there is some scheme in the wind for cleaning up the drugs racket in Deniston but I don't know how far it's developed yet, nor any details of it. Sometimes a small operator can lead to the Big Fish, you know. Maybe the authorities would prefer not to crack down on The Groove yet. I don't know. At any rate, you have told what you suspect to me, officially. I'll work on from there.'

She glanced at her watch and prepared to rise, but Ted Blake's cool voice stayed her.

'Miss Sheldon hasn't told us yet why she was at The Groove this evening.'

'She's told me, and it's a private matter,' Dave replied quickly. 'So I don't think you should ask her, Sexton, boy.'

Brenda settled herself into her chair again. 'D'you know,' she said, 'I've been so interested in your story I'd quite forgotten my own part in tonight's business. As I told Dave earlier, I was at that cafe hoping to see a young man who, I believe, goes there. I want to find out who he is, and for certain reasons I can't act officially in the matter.' She paused, then went on hopefully. 'He's about seventeen or eighteen, tall, thin, brownish hair and a big nose. And he has a round birthmark at an angle of his jaw, on the right side of his face.'

'Does he ride a push bike?' Johnny asked at once.

Brenda swirled round on him, her eyes flashing.

'He does. You know him, Johnny?'

'We ain't bosom friends, miss, in fact, I've only spoken to him once, but I can tell you his name and address.'

He thrust his left hand inside his jacket and seemed to grope in the top inner pocket. Then he withdrew his hand, showing an empty palm, the fingers close together. He frowned, turned his hand over and studied the back of it.

'That's funny,' he muttered. 'Had it just now. Musta parked it somewhere. Ah, of course, I remember!' He reached sideways and produced, apparently from Ted Blake's ear, an oblong of white printed card.

Dave Morgan chuckled. 'Johnny Pitts, the great illusionist and man of magic, look you. But he's good, Miss Sheldon. Has a natural gift for conjuring.'

Johnny got up, pushed past Ted and handed Brenda the card, grinning modestly. She looked at the front of it. In ornate script it was headed, 'St Faith's Youth Recreation Centre. Membership Card.' There were lines to carry a name and address, and below, times and days when the centre was open. Brenda's eyes fixed on two handwritten lines — 'Arnold Toller, The Laurels, 6 Belsize Avenue, Deniston 16.'

'How did you get this, Johnny?' she asked.

'Remember Sexton told you I followed a character out of The Groove on Saturday night? This was the feller. He disappeared into a narrow space between a coupla houses, and when I got there he was wheeling this bike out, seemed to be

64

in a hurry, too. So I stepped into his way, accidental, like, and stumbled into his front wheel, falling forward and grabbing him — I had to, di'n't I, to keep me balance? I wanted to find out who he was if I could and when I grabbed him I lifted his wallet. Thing I've practiced for hours. Well, then I reckoned the wheel had caught me in the — that's to say, miss, where it hurts like nobody's business, and I doubled meself up, turning away from him, and I managed to open the wallet, saw the top of this card, and nicked it. I put the wallet back in his pocket while he was apologizing and soothing me down, like.'

'May I keep this, Johnny?'

'Sure, miss, if it's any use to you. You can have this as well, if you like.' From a side pocket he produced a handsome pigskin notecase, with the initials 'E.B.' across one corner in gilt lettering.

'Why, you — !' Ted Blake sprang up, clapping a hand to his hip pocket. Then he grinned as he reached out for his property.

'You can't stop him,' he said. 'It's

become a mania with him. I'd advise you to check your shoe laces before you leave, Miss Sheldon.'

Brenda laughed as she got up and wished them all goodnight. Dave murmured he'd see her to her car, but Brenda shook her head. 'No need for that, thanks,' she said and went quickly out of the room and down the stairs, after promising to keep in touch with Dave, to let him know of any further developments.

A full moon was up now, the court bathed in its light. Brenda caught a glimpse of a man's figure dodging through the entrance, towards the street, as she stepped out into the court. But in the street itself there was no movement. It was deserted except for three cars, her own, Ted's, and a dark-coloured Vauxhall parked some distance from the other two. Brenda got into her own car to drive home.

It was after ten o'clock now and the traffic was light. She had heard a car start up from behind her as she turned out of Duncan Street, her mind registered the fact but gave it no significance. Neither did she notice the car which passed along the street where she lived just as she was driving into her own garage.

She went into the house and sat down to the laden supper tray her mother brought from the kitchen. Mrs Sheldon didn't ask Brenda where she had been nor what she had done; as the mother of a woman detective-constable she was used to her daughter's irregular comings and goings.

'Did you ring the hospital again?' Brenda asked.

'I did, and such a nice ward sister answered. Gertrude's doing very well, she's fully conscious and there's no really serious damage done. But she's not at all clear what happened, it's a loss of memory the sister says will be only temporary, and everything will come back to her in a day or two. Because of this, they've told Mr Joynton it's useless to keep one of his policewomen hanging around the hospital. And we can go to see her tomorrow afternoon.'

Brenda ate her supper thoughtfully.

She'd have to get in touch with Mr Hallam, or possibly with his second-in-command, Chief Detective-Inspector 'Jack' Spratt, and give them Dave Morgan's suspicions of The Groove Cafe. But it was late to try to contact either of them tonight. Tomorrow would surely do.

She put her tray aside, went into the hall and picked up the telephone directory to look up the name and address Johnny Pitts had given her. Toller, R. G. was the name in the directory, which would be the youth's father. She went back into the lounge.

'The name Toller seems to ring a bell with me, mum,' she said. 'Does it with you?'

'There's a Robert Toller on the city council,' her mother responded promptly. 'He represents North-West Division.'

Brenda thanked her. Sometimes it was useful to have a mother who was a keen student of local politics.

5

The following day was a Wednesday, half-day closing at Mrs Avery's shop. Brenda's mother, who was really enjoying herself as a businesswoman, told her daughter she wouldn't need any counter assistance that morning. She went off just before eight o'clock to open the shop, and Brenda, having cleared away and washed up their breakfast things, decided to wait until nine before ringing Chief Superintendent Hallam. He was usually at his desk on the stroke of that hour.

She was glancing through the morning paper when the telephone began to shrill a summons. Brenda picked up the receiver, gave her number.

'Is that you, now, Miss Sheldon?' she heard. 'Dave Morgan here, look you. Last night you said you were going to call your headquarters, wasn't it, to tell your boss about — well, you know. You done that, then?'

'Not yet. I wanted to speak directly to my chief, who comes on duty at nine. Why do you ask?'

'Well, something important's come up, you see. Something you should know before you ring him. Might make a lot of difference. Now, look, Miss Sheldon, I can't talk about this on the phone. And it was wondering, I was, if you would come down to the gym in Duncan Street this morning, so we could discuss it there?'

'Yes, I could do that, Dave. What time?'

'Soon as ever you can. I'll be waiting in the office for you.'

Brenda glanced at her wrist-watch. 'It's eight-forty now. I could be there by a quarter past nine.'

'That would do fine. Expecting you, I'll be.'

She heard the click of a replaced receiver, put her own back on its studs and stood looking absently at it, her brows drawn in a frown. The voice had sounded like Dave Morgan's, and yet there had been a difference. It had been *too* Welsh, both in phrasing and accent. Then she recollected that regional accents are usually emphasized over the telephone.

Satisfied on this point, she got herself ready, locked up the house and drove to Duncan Street. It was a short street, with a shop on each corner. Warehouses, a disused chapel, a pub and the high walls of a school playground were all it served, and at this time of the morning it was empty save for the Vauxhall — in daylight she saw its colour was maroon — which had been there the previous evening. It was now parked almost across the entrance of the court which led to Dave's gym. She decided it must be the Welshman's car.

She drew up behind it, locked her vehicle and walked across the court. At the head of the stairs she could see the office door, partly open, and as she mounted, with her shoes clicking on the bare treads, a cheerful voice rose from inside the office.

'That you, Miss Sheldon? Come right in please.'

Brenda pushed the door open, took a pace forward — and then everything seemed to happen. A pair of large rough hands grabbed her wrists from behind, pulling her arms back, pinioning them. At the same time a cloth bag was forced down over her head. She gasped for breath in its folds and tasted dust and fluff. Her handbag went flying, she kicked out wildly but met no resistance. A voice spoke close to her ear.

'You've two choices, lady. Take it easy, and you'll be glad for the rest of your life that you did. Give us trouble, and you'll wish you hadn't. There's three of us here, so, like you cops say, you'd better come quietly.'

The tones were harsh, menacing. The man who held her arms gave them a sudden upwards jerk and Brenda gasped in pain.

She felt more hands at her ankles. They were being tied, but not tightly, together. She was being hobbled, like a horse. The man who was doing it spoke lewdly. Brenda could imagine his lecherous grin.

'Smashing legs this bird has. I wouldn't mind — '

'Cut that out!' It was the first voice

again. 'We've no time to play around. Up on your feet and tie these bag-tapes round under her chin.'

'Okay, Chuck. She won't suffocate, will she? I reckon we ought to keep a check on that. How's about if I have me hand on her heart, so if it feels it's going to stop I can warn you?'

Brenda heard the smack of an open hand against flesh. 'Next time it'll be my fist,' the other growled, 'and you'll be spitting teeth.'

The silent one of the trio, he who held her arms, suddenly pulled them down behind her. There was a click and she felt the coldness of steel against her wrists. She was shoved forward and pushed into a chair.

'Listen,' said the man who had been called Chuck. 'I'm going down to make sure all's clear. You, Smedley, will come with me to the bottom of the stairs. When I give you the all right you'll come back up here and help Buster to bring her to the car.'

Brenda heard the sound of his retreating footsteps. She hadn't the least idea what this was all about; it was uncomfortable, but not painful, to be immobilized as she was, and, now she had become a little used to it, she found she could breathe fairly well inside the cloth bag. She was going to be taken away from here, that was obvious, and she couldn't do much about it. She remembered the court was not overlooked by windows, she could be rushed across it and forced into a car — the Vauxhall, she guessed — without much risk to her captors. They hadn't gagged her, but she doubted if screaming, yelling for help, would do much good. A muffled voice doesn't carry very far, and, most likely, there wouldn't be anyone around to hear her. Best to play this thing along, and see where it led.

Footsteps again, coming upstairs. 'Okay,' said the voice of Smedley, the man who had fixed her ankles. The other one, he who had been called Buster, grunted.

'Look, lady.' His voice was hoarse, its accent uncultured. 'You don't want trouble, we don't want trouble. So use your loaf and you won't get any — see?'

Brenda didn't bother to reply as she

was jerked to her feet. With a man on each side of her grasping a shoulder, she was guided out to the landing. The cords at her ankles allowed her to take short, shuffling steps.

'Now the stairs.' It was Buster's gravelly voice again. 'We'll see you don't fall. Feel for the first 'un and you'll be okay.'

With nothing to cling to, Brenda moved very gingerly and Buster growled at her to hurry up. The other man, Smedley, chuckled evilly.

'Maybe we'd better carry her,' he said. 'You go first and take her head and I'll see to the other end.'

'Might be a good idea, at that,' Buster agreed, whereupon Brenda's pace improved considerably. There wasn't room on the stairs for three of them abreast, Buster dropped back, and as he did so he muttered to his captive.

'Thought that 'ud hurry you, girlie. I don't blame you. If I was a bird I 'oodn't want Smedley's dirty hands anywhere around me. We're nearly at the bottom of the stairs now.'

They came to level ground, Brenda was

steered quickly across the court. Her nostrils caught a faint smell of oil and car upholstery. Somebody — she thought it was Chuck — said, 'One step up, now.' She took it, stumbling forward and sideways to slump in a heap on a car seat. As she wriggled upright, one of the men got in beside her. Then came the closing of two doors, the car started up and moved away. Brenda realized she wasn't in her own vehicle and the man at her side, who was Buster by his voice, croaked out, 'Don't worry about that Triumph of yours. The other bloke's bringing it on.' Brenda didn't answer. She was trying to concentrate on the route they were taking.

The car turned right at the end of Duncan Street. That meant they were headed southwards, away from the centre of the city. If they maintained that direction, they would pass through a rather dreary district of factories and streets with small, grimy houses. She moved slightly to her left and her shoulder came up against what seemed to be a piece of hardboard. Beneath the cover over her head she smiled grimly. Obviously, the left hand rear window of the Vauxhall had been blocked to prevent observation from passers-by, who might become curious if they saw the grotesque thing she was wearing; from the rear it would merely look like some sort of hood. And on the other side, the man Buster would screen her.

The fellow they had called Chuck — Johnny Pitts had heard that name at The Groove the previous evening — was driving. He was handling the Vauxhall expertly, Brenda sensed he was travelling as fast as the speed limit would allow, but taking no chances at all. Once they stopped momentarily, probably for traffic lights, she thought, but the fact was no help to her. There were several sets of lights on this way out of town. For all she knew, Chuck might have gone through one or more already, coming up to them on the green.

The car slowed, turned left, then left again after a brief interval. The next turn was to the right, a left turn followed, two rights succeeded that. Brenda relaxed.

The idea was clearly to confuse her so completely that she wouldn't ever be able to back-track the route she was being driven over. Well, that plan had worked, she hadn't the faintest idea now where she was.

She said loudly, 'Can't I have the fastenings on this ridiculous bag thing loosened? I'm choking to death inside it.'

Chuck's voice came from the driver's seat. 'Do what she says, mate. But don't take it right off. And first check those cuffs are still working. They weren't made for women's wrists.'

Buster's thick fingers fiddled behind her at the handcuffs, then the tapes of her hood were undone, the bottom of it pulled loose. She could breathe more freely now, and talk more clearly, too. Maybe a little conversation at this point would pay, now or later.

'This is a stupid idea, if ever there was one,' she said. 'I don't know what you're up to, but you're going to regret it.'

Neither of the men made a reply.

'Of course,' she went on chattily, 'I wasn't very bright myself, falling for that fake phone call. I thought at the time it wasn't really Dave Morgan's voice. But you know how it is, you take a chance sometimes. Not such a chance as you lot are taking, though. In fact, chance is the wrong word there. Still, maybe I shouldn't be warning you — you've asked for it.'

Beside her, Buster stirred uneasily. She felt him lean forward.

'What's she on about, mate? I don't like it.'

The driver replied with a harsh chuckle. 'She's trying to kid us, boy. That's all it is. Don't listen to her.'

'Please yourselves,' Brenda said. 'I'm only trying to do you both a good turn. That other man — Smedley, isn't it? — wanted to take the chance, when you had me helpless, to mess about with me a bit. And you wouldn't let him. I'm grateful for that. Not that Smedley matters. If he hasn't been picked up in my car by now, he will be, any minute.' She paused, a little breathlessly. If Smedley were tailing them, that card wouldn't take a trick. But she didn't think he would be. Chuck had used a devious route to confuse her; it was likely her own car would be driven direct to some rendezvous.

Buster was moving uneasily again. She knew her guess was right.

'What about that, Chuck? If she's talking turkey, we're clean in it. Smedley'll sing as soon as the fuzz fingers him, and you know it.'

The Vauxhall slowed and came to a halt. The engine was silenced and Brenda heard the driver shift in his seat.

'Listen, copper.' His voice was so clear she knew he must have turned round to face her. 'You might as well know the score. I rang your pad this morning — right? Then I rang again when I thought you'd have set off for Morgan's place. No reply, so you had. Then I phoned your headquarters at Kingsmead House. Gave a duff name, of course. Said I'd some special information for you, wanted to speak to you. Switchboard girl said you were on leave. I asked if you had rung in this morning. You hadn't. Okay, you'd not changed your mind and got in touch with any of your bosses. And, because I'm a fellow who likes to cover every angle, I then rang your mother at that shop. We had your house watched this morning, you see, and she was tailed there. Right. So I tell the old lady I'm calling from your headquarters to say you'd been fetched back off leave for special duty and I'd been told to let her know. The old girl swallowed it, said that happened all the time. I warned her you'd likely be going out of town, so to expect you again when she saw you. Got all that? So now you know it all, you can stop scaring my pal here out of his tiny mind.'

The engine fired again and the car moved smoothly off.

Brenda set her lips. Her bluff hadn't worked. But while Chuck had been speaking she had listened hard, and not only to him. They had pulled up on a country road, that was obvious. She had heard the lowing of a cow nearby and not far away a tractor was working. No vehicles had passed them while they had been halted. It was clear they were now well away from any urban area. If they

81

had continued to travel south, as she suspected they had, they were now in a district of rolling farmland, a region soon to have the quietness it had enjoyed for centuries devastated by the new motorway which was advancing northwards, casually bulldozing fields, cottages, farmhouses, out of its persistent way.

The Vauxhall turned sharply right and at once the wheels began to bump along a rough, uneven surface. Then the car pulled up with a jerk and she heard Chuck get out. There was the click of a gate latch, a murmur of voices. Chuck re-entered the car and drove it slowly forwards for a short distance. Then he stopped, pulled on the hand brake, cut the engine.

'Here we are,' he grunted to Buster. 'Let's get her out.'

'What about this thing on her nut?' Buster enquired. 'How about taking it off now? Make things easy for one and all.'

'She's to stay blind till we get inside,' Chuck answered. 'That's the order. Come on, get moving.'

Brenda was jerked to her feet, Buster's

hands on her shoulders pulled her forward. She stumbled out of the car, steadied by Chuck. Her feet found a hard level surface which she judged was concrete. A faint farmyard smell stole into her nostrils.

She was guided along a paved path. There was the rattle of a doorlatch, the squeal and scrape of an ill-hung door moving reluctantly on unoiled hinges. Then she was pushed forward, the door shut behind her. 'Okay now,' Chuck said. 'Take it off.'

Buster's fingers fumbled, and then light struck her eyes and made her blink. Her vision adjusted quickly, for the room in which they stood had but one window and this was roughly boarded up, with light coming only through crannies between the wood. The room itself was bare of furniture, there was a rusting range built into one of its walls, the floor was littered with rubbish — straw, crumpled pieces of paper, broken boxes and torn cartons. The ceiling was beamed, and carried hooks; she recognized the place as a deserted farm kitchen. Chuck stepped behind her, there was a metallic click and she found her arms were free.

She rubbed at her wrists for some moments to restore their sluggish circulation, then put her hands to her mussed-up hair. Chuck, facing her now, nodded to Buster, who knelt down to free her ankles. Looking down at his broad back, she realized he was even bigger than she had thought. He stood upright, towering over her, a huge man with a small round head which didn't fit his massive shoulders at all. His nose was flattened, his mouth showed the gaps of missing teeth. Looking at his eyes, she saw they were deep-set, piggy. Not a man of great intelligence, she judged.

Chuck was the wiry man with protruding teeth whom she had dealt with at The Groove the previous evening. He had seemed a tough character then, and now the sinister grin on his face underlined her estimate of him.

But she regarded them both coolly enough and said, 'Well, what's the next move in this silly game?'

Buster grunted and Chuck crossed to the window to peer through one of the chinks of its boards.

'Ah,' he said, 'I see Smedley's got here with her car. So that's worked out okay.' Brenda noticed he had her handbag tucked under one arm. He swung away from the window to add, 'Watch her, Buster, and if she makes any sort of a wrong move, smack her down. As soon as Smedley comes in, I'll go upstairs and find out what the boss wants us to do next.' He added, to Brenda, 'And don't try any of your fancy judo tricks on him. He's been an all-in wrestler, and he's forgotten more holds and throws than you've ever heard of. Smedley'll have the time of his life if Buster finds it necessary to stand you on your head and hold you like that.'

Smedley came crabwise into the kitchen and grinned greasily. 'No problems,' he said. 'Only, we'd better shove the Vaux into one of them barns. It's plain in view from the road.'

'See to it, then.' Chuck handed him keys. 'And put this bird's car alongside it.'

Smedley nodded, went out again. Chuck crossed the kitchen, opened a door in the far wall and Brenda heard him climb a flight of uncarpeted stairs. Buster licked his lips, his small eyes never leaving Brenda's face.

'Take my advice and be'ave yerself,' he growled. 'I don't like hurting women, but, by God, I'll hurt you if you give trouble.'

Brenda didn't reply. She was listening to the murmur of voices in a room overhead. They ceased, and Chuck's footsteps sounded again on the stairs. He stepped into the kitchen and jerked his head at Brenda.

'Come on, up aloft, and watch it. I'll be right behind you, with this.' His hand darted beneath his coat, came out holding a long, keen-bladed throwing knife. 'Two inches of this in your kidneys, beautiful, and you'll die a proper messy death. Now move yourself!'

6

The stairs were dirty, their treads scarred and splintered. They rose to a small square landing with three doors. Two of these were closed. The third was hanging crookedly from its hinges but it had been pushed back and the windows of the room beyond were uncovered. Brenda was prodded into this room. Ancient paper, half peeled from its walls, showed cracks in the filthy plaster beneath, the floorboards were rough, caked here and there with mud. A rusting, abandoned bed-frame in a corner was heaped with old clothes, broken picture frames, a pair of manure-smeared cracked gumboots.

In the centre of the room a baize-covered card table was set up and behind it, in a tubular steel canvas-covered chair, a woman was sitting. She looked up from the papers she was studying as Brenda and her escort appeared, and crushed out a cigarette into a chipped saucer which was overflowing with ash and filter-tipped stubs.

She was tall, slenderly built, with a small mouth and a pointed chin. The coal-black, bouffant wig she was wearing did not match her hard, pale-blue eyes, over which thick black eyebrows had been painted. She wore a plain grey dress, unrelieved by any jewellery, her narrow feet were in flat-heeled shoes. Brenda glanced at her hands. The long fingers were nicotine-stained. Her left hand bore a wedding ring of thin platinum. She returned Brenda's glance coolly as she swept the table clear of her papers, pushing them into a box file which lay on another canvas chair beside her. She closed the file, lifted it on to the table and pushed the empty chair forward with a thrust of one foot.

'You can sit down if you wish,' she said. Her voice was unaccented, cold and flat.

'Thanks, Mrs Whoever-you-are,' Brenda returned, 'but I prefer to stand.'

The woman shrugged. 'Suit yourself. And my name, Miss Sheldon, is Lingford, Vera Lingford.'

'You'll have a criminal record, no doubt?' Brenda wasn't feeling at all happy with the situation she'd got herself into, but she didn't mean to let these people see her state of mind.

'We'll by-pass the chit-chat,' Mrs Lingford said acidly. 'I have some questions to ask you and the answers had better be correct.' She looked beyond Brenda at Chuck. 'You can stay,' she told him. 'I'd like you to hear what she has to say.'

Chuck nodded, looked affectionately at the knife he still held, then slid it out of sight and stepped sideways to lean against a wall. 'She's said nothing to us yet,' he grunted.

The woman lit another cigarette, took a long drag at it, expelled smoke from between her thin lips.

'Now, Woman Detective-Constable Sheldon,' she began. 'You were at The Groove Cafe last night. I understand you were there unofficially, looking for a youth named Arnold Toller. Correct?'

'If you say so.'

'Oh, come on, now, don't let's play it

coy. What is your interest in young Toller? I might be able to help you, you know.'

Brenda considered a moment, but she couldn't see any harm in answering the question.

'We think it's possible he may be connected with holding up a shopkeeper with intent to rob, and causing the shopkeeper serious injury.'

'You're trying to mislead me.' The words were snapped out. 'You say 'we' as if you were acting last night in your official capacity. We know you were there for private reasons. I want to know what those were.'

'I don't choose to give them.'

Mrs Lingford's painted eyebrows rose. 'In that case, I shall have to give them to you myself. I know, you see. I was merely asking you as a double check on my information. The shopkeeper who was attacked — Mrs Avery — is a great friend of yours. I've had enquiries made, you understand. I don't know why you weren't put on the case officially, but that doesn't matter. It's clear to me you wanted a bit of personal revenge in the matter of Toller. You went to The Groove for that purpose. And quite by chance you stumbled on — er — certain activities there. You haven't reported these yet.'

'Which is why, I suppose, I've been abducted and brought here?'

'Exactly. And you will be kept here until I give the order to let you go. That will be when I have made arrangements to reorganize my business in Deniston. The Groove Cafe constituted only a very small cell in the project with which I'm concerned, it is now eliminated and if and when your people search the place, they will find no evidence. By then we shall have moved on, quite out of your reach.

'Now, Miss Sheldon, I advise you to be co-operative. That way, no harm will come to you. But if you do anything foolish, I promise you you'll suffer. You might even be put out of the way altogether, and I mean that. It's a contingency I hope to avoid, since a corpse is always an awkward object to deal with. I trust I've made myself clear?'

'You've certainly talked a lot.' Brenda

replied. 'I won't try to tell you what I think of you and the dirty game you're playing. But you won't get away with it, you know. We'll deal with you, sooner or later.'

Mrs Lingford laughed mockingly. 'It's extremely good of you to warn me. However, I fear this pleasant chat must come to an end. I have a great deal to do today.' She turned to Chuck, who was still leaning against the wall. 'Call that gorilla up here, will you?'

Chuck stepped to the door and shouted, 'Hi, Buster!' and the big man came lumbering up the stairs and into the room. Mrs Lingford nodded at Brenda. 'Just watch her, my man. You can rough her up a little if she doesn't behave. Chuck, you come and help me.'

She got up and crossed to the old bed in the corner. With Chuck's assistance, she began to clear it of the rubbish it bore. Brenda stayed where she was, with Buster immobile behind her, standing just out of reach of a backward kick, or a sudden whirl and tackle which wouldn't give him room to counter. But Brenda had no intention of trying a break. These were ruthless, iron-hard people. She knew she had read the woman correctly. Mrs Lingford would allow nothing, nobody, to get in her way. She, Brenda, could only play along with them, and hope for the best.

There was some muttering from the corner by the bed. Chuck seemed to be receiving orders. He nodded and went downstairs, while Mrs Lingford strolled to the window, looking out, standing in a patch of sunlight, for the day was one of those in late October which, beginning misty and cool, turn out into brilliant sunshine with summer heat in it still.

Chuck came upstairs again, a stout cord dangling from his hands. 'Over here with her, Buster,' he commanded, but before the big man could touch her, Brenda walked forward and, nonchalantly enough, lay down on the rusty bed-springs. 'This is the idea, I suppose?' she said and Mrs Lingford's hard mouth widened in a brief smile.

'Sensible, at any rate,' she commented. 'There's nothing like a little collaboration to make things easier all round.' But she stood watching Brenda vigilantly while Chuck tied the captive's wrists and ankles expertly to the bed frame, testing the knots, the rope's tightness, with care. He straightened his back. 'How about that?' he asked. 'There's enough left to tie her down across the middle.' But the woman shook her head.

'Remember, Buster will be watching her all the time. Go and get that old chair.' She stepped to the table, opened the shiny handbag which stood on it. She took out a spool of surgical tape, which she handed to Buster.

'She can scream her head off and nobody will hear her,' she said with a jerk of the chin towards the captive. 'But if she does so, it won't be very pleasant for you, so here's something to tape her lips with. Now, Chuck and I will clear up and get off. Smedley's on guard outside. We'll be back as soon as we can, say two hours at the most, and we'll all leave here tonight.' She broke off as Chuck came in, carrying a battered wooden armchair. 'Here's something for you to park on,' she added.

Buster looked at the watch he wore on a thick, hairy wrist.

'It's getting on for me dinnertime,' he said plaintively. 'When do I get to eat?'

'There are sandwiches and drinks in the car boot,' Mrs Lingford replied. 'I'll leave them out downstairs before we go. You'll share them with Smedley.'

'Okay, missus.' Buster looked somewhat happier. He sat down gingerly in the chair while Chuck folded up the table and the two small chairs. Mrs Lingford picked up the box file.

'We'll see you later, then,' she said and she and Chuck went downstairs. There were movements there for a while and then Brenda heard a car start up and drive off. She spoke from the bed.

'I wouldn't like to be in your shoes, Buster, when the law catches up on you. People in your game get long stretches these days.'

'If they're caught,' Buster growled. 'And the missus'll see we ain't. So not to worry.'

'The big shot, is she? What's the size of the territory she's operating?'

'Look, miss.' Buster moved impatiently. 'I ain't one for gabbing, and 'specially now. So can it, willya? Let's have a bit of quiet.'

'Whatever you say.' Brenda wriggled into as comfortable a position as she could and closed her eyes, trying to relax. The room was close and stuffy and she began to feel rather sleepy. Maybe forty winks wouldn't do her any harm. She drifted into a light doze.

The scrape of chair legs over the rough floor brought her into alertness again. Buster was on his feet. He walked across to her, tested her bonds, then went thumping down the stairs. He was back almost at once, carrying a crate of bottled beer. A large paper packet was tucked under one of his arms. He put his burdens down by his chair, sat down, opened a bottle of beer and drank it noisily.

'That's better,' he said, and opened a second bottle. 'How about a sup, miss? Plenty here for all.'

Brenda shook her head. 'I don't care for beer, thanks.'

'Pity. This is good stuff.' He put the bottle to his lips and liquid disappeared, gurgling, like water down a drain. He returned the empty bottle to the crate, picked up a third, looked at it doubtfully then, muttering, 'Might as well,' he drank it dry, more slowly this time. Then he unwrapped the paper packet, revealing a pile of sandwiches. He took one off the top of the pile, produced a big claspknife from his pocket and sawed the sandwich in half.

'If you was feeling a bit peckish, miss, I could feed you one o' these, in bits, like.'

'I'm all right, thank you.' Brenda didn't fancy his thick fingers shoving food into her mouth. 'You go ahead and enjoy yourself — while you can.'

Buster had no reply to this. Brenda raised her head and watched him wolf down half-a-dozen sandwiches before he put the rest of the food on the floor, laid his knife beside it and reached for another bottle of beer. He swilled this down, with a second to follow it. Then he stretched out in his chair, his feet stuck forward, his head resting against the wooden back, his hands folded on his capacious stomach. Clearly, he was feeling the soporific effects of the food and drink, and the room was even warmer, closer, now. His eyelids drooped, his breathing became heavy.

Once again Brenda tested her bonds, as she had done at intervals. They were still fast — no hope at all of getting them loose. Buster emitted a strangled snore, jerked in his chair and then relaxed again.

Brenda wondered where the other man, Smedley, was. Keeping a look-out downstairs, she supposed. At any moment he'd be up here for his food and drink. When he appeared, she meant to rouse Buster, who was now fast asleep. She didn't fancy being a helpless victim to Smedley's attentions.

From the direction of the open door came a hissing sound, repeated urgently. Brenda's head came up again.

A teenage girl stood there, looking at her. She was tall, black-haired, with large dark eyes, her clothes were rumpled and stained, her shoes scuffed. She looked desperately in need of a wash. Staring back at her, Brenda knew she had seen her before somewhere, and the spark of recognition in the girl's eyes made that knowledge definite. Then Brenda remembered. As a woman constable at Deniston Central, where she had worked before her transfer to Regional, she had had the task of returning this young madam and one of her friends to Westwood Approved School, from which they had absconded. Her name was . . . Yes, Elsie Thompson. Her friend had been called Jean Hathorn.

The girl tip-toed into the room, sliding along by the wall, her eyes never once leaving Buster's sleeping form. Without so much as a whisper, she bent to examine the cords which bound Brenda's ankles. Her long-nailed fingers tried the knots. She shook her head dubiously.

Brenda said in a murmur of sound, 'The knife, by his chair, on the packet.' Elsie Thompson nodded, turned and crawled on hands and knees towards Buster. She removed the claspknife without even a rustle of paper, crawled back and began to use it, swiftly and expertly. Four slashes from the honed blade, and Brenda was free.

She rolled carefully off the bed, taking care to raise the minimum of noise from the rusty mattress springs. Buster was deep in a snoring session as Brenda stood up, swaying a little as pins and needles attacked her feet and legs. Elsie grabbed her hand.

'Come on, follow me, quick!' She slid out of the room as she had entered it. She was still carrying Buster's open knife. On the landing she turned to her right, pushed open a door which stood ajar and led Brenda into another empty room. A smaller girl — yes, it was Jean Hathorn again — was crouched beneath a windowsill, looking out. She got up, stared at Brenda.

'Why, it's that woman scuffer as — ' she began, but Elsie cut her short.

'Shut yer damn great trap and let's all get the hell outa here!' she whispered hoarsely. There was a second door in one corner of the room, towards which the two girls hurried. It opened upon a short passage, with a flight of rough stairs at its end.

Still somewhat bemused, Brenda followed the pair down the stairs into what seemed to be a combined back kitchen and dairy. They crossed to an outer door, and through it on to a small paved courtyard. Elsie swung to face Brenda.

'Look, miss. There's a car — one of these Triumphs — in a barn what's got no door. We'd 'a' pinched it if we could have drove the blasted thing. But you'll know how to drive, o' course.'

'I do, and the Triumph's my car. Only, I haven't got the ignition key. It was taken from me.'

'What crummy luck! Well, we'd better get somewhere outa sight before that big ape yonder wakes up!'

Jean Hathorn spoke for the first time. 'Stable loft again? Under that old pile of sacks, eh? They'll never think of looking there.'

'Might be an idea.' Elsie was about to dart across the yard when Brenda grasped her thin shoulder.

'Wait a minute. There's another man around somewhere watching out. We don't want to run into him.'

Elsie laughed hoarsely, and Jean giggled.

'You mean a little runt with brown hair all in patches, like a rat with the mange?' Elsie asked.

'That's him. The others called him Smedley.'

'So not to worry,' Elsie said. 'We've got him, laid out cold. It's a bit of a long story. Look, let's get outa here, into the stable. Safer there.'

She led the way out of the courtyard. They dodged between a sagging cowshed and an abandoned piggery, crossed another yard with a grass-grown manure heap in the middle of it, and reached a gap-roofed building with a door hanging loosely on rusty hinges. They squeezed past its narrow opening to be greeted by a faint smell of horses and harness leather.

'We're okay here,' Elsie said. 'Look, you can climb on to that manger, pull yerself through the gap above it and you're in the loft. Jean, you keep watch behind that door.'

She settled herself on a rat-gnawed corn bin and grinned at Brenda through her long hair.

'You know us, of course, miss. You and another she-dick took us back to Westwood when we scarpered from there before. Right. Well, we decided, Jean and me, to have another little holiday, like. We dropped across this old farm, I reckon it's been left like this because of that new motorway what's coming across here. We hadn't been here more'n a few minutes when up drove this car and a woman got out with this fellow whatsisname, the one I quietened, and they go inside the farmhouse, see? Then that big bloke upstairs comes along in another car with a pal and in they go too. They was in there for quite a while, mebbe an hour, and meanwhile Jean and me had found this good place in the loft yonder.' She jerked a thumb.

'Well, in the end they all comes out and drives off. That 'ud be just before dark last night. Me and Jean got into the farmhouse by the back door, which was open. We give the place a proper going over but there wasn't nothing to be seen except a lotta fag butts in that room where we found you. But we thought it wasn't a good idea to sleep in the 'ouse, case they came back.

'Well, they didn't, not then, but this tall bird turns up early this morning. We was just thinking of moving on ourselves when you and your boy friends turned up. We couldn't see who you was, of course, being as 'ow your nut was all covered up, but we was int'rested and thought we'd see what went on. Anything doing out there, Jean?'

'Quiet as the flipping grave, Else.'

'Keep on looking. Well, as I say, we see them go in and then this runt, what had drove up a bit previous in another car, comes out and starts poking about the yard. And stone me if he didn't walk straight into here. We see him coming, so Jean makes a dash for the loft, only she gets stuck somehow and we was proper caught. Lucky for us, I'd found this in one of the sheds the night before, and I had it ready.'

She stooped, and from the other side of the corn bin she produced a pick handle, worn, but still serviceable.

'Me brother taught me how to use one

of these, miss. I know just where and how hard to hit to put a bloke to sleep for quite a while. Which reminds me. Better see how he's going on.'

She slid from the bin, walked to a dimly-lit corner of the stable and swung open the wooden door of a box stall. Brenda followed her. On the rotting straw inside the stall lay the crumpled body of Smedley.

'Has he croaked yet?' Jean asked casually from her post.

'Shouldn't have.' Elsie knelt down, her head to Smedley's chest. 'No, he's all right. Still out, though. But he'll be round any time now.' She got up and turned to Brenda again.

'Then we thinks it 'ud be a good idea to see what was going on inside. So we goes quietly up the back stairs, and who should I see but you?'

'And you rescued me, Elsie. How come? You don't like coppers.'

'Aw, well.' The girl looked at her feet. 'You know when we was fingered before, and you took us back? You told the old bag as runs Westwood we'd given no trouble and not to be hard on us. And I reckoned we owed you something. And as for not liking coppers, I'm not so sure about that now. If I could be one like you, miss, I reckon if I could have the chance to join up . . . '

Brenda gave her shoulder a quick squeeze. 'I'm not a policewoman today, Elsie. Officially, I haven't seen you. Of course, you're bound to be caught again, sooner or later, but at the moment I think we three had better get out of this place.' A sudden thought struck her, and she poked Smedley's body with the toe of her shoe. 'This man will probably have my car keys on him. Search him, will you?'

Elsie nodded, dropping on her knees again. Smedley was certainly coming back to life, he was twitching spasmodically and now and then he uttered a deep groan.

'Here you are, miss!' Brenda took the keys Elsie held out. 'And your car's in a barn — we'll show you!'

They hurried across the yard. The barn doors were open, they were in sight of the window of the room in which Brenda had been held, but all seemed peaceful there still. Brenda pushed the two girls into the Triumph and slid behind the wheel. The engine fired at a touch and then they were away, bumping along the neglected track with, before them, freedom and safety.

The gate at the end of the track was closed. Brenda halted the car and Elsie jumped out to open the gate. At that moment a heavily-built, dark-browed man, in rough tweeds and a cap, stepped from behind the massive trunk of an oak tree which overshadowed the gate. There was a sporting rifle in his hands.

'And where the 'ell do you think you're going?' he demanded.

7

Brenda's hands tightened on the wheel of her car and behind her Jean Hathorn gave a squawk of dismay. But Elsie Thompson did not seem unduly perturbed.

'We're going through this gate,' she said. 'And if you were any sort of a gent you'd open it for us.'

The man brought the rifle forward. 'Stay where you are. Don't move. And you — the other girl — let's have a look at you. Come on, now!'

Elsie turned her head. 'Get out, Jean, like he says. We don't want to be mixed up in anything, do we? Stone the crows, we don't.' She giggled. 'Silly thing to say, ain't it — stone the crows? Don't seem to be any crows hereabouts, though there's bags of stones on this flaming cart-track, ain't there, Jean?'

Jean said loudly, 'You bet.' She opened the car door and got out, stumbling as she did so. She lurched forward, then snatched up a jagged stone and flung it hard at the man with the rifle. He ducked to avoid it and like a flash the two girls were round the oak tree and running like greyhounds along the hedge beyond it. At the far end of the field was a wood, sanctuary to them. The man recovered his balance, swung his rifle to his shoulder. The action was instinctive and Brenda, out of the car now, sprang forward with a cry of 'No! Don't shoot!' The man turned on her at once.

'Get back into that car, you!' His voice grated harshly. 'Do as I say, or you'll get a bullet in your foot.' Brenda pulled herself up. She saw he meant it. She turned her head at a shout from behind. Buster was lumbering down the track from the farm, moving at a surprising speed for one of his bulk. He looked distinctly annoyed.

She shrugged, accepting the situation. The gate was still closed, she couldn't break it by charging her car at it. If she tried anything of the sort, the man with the rifle could put a shot into one of her tyres . . . He was watching her carefully. She turned to the car and took her place behind the wheel.

Buster came charging up. 'You got her, did you?' he panted. 'She got free somehow, how the hell I don't know.' He peered at the now-distant figures of the two girls. 'Who's them, then?'

'A couple of kids who were with her,' the other man grunted. 'Probably helped her to escape. They got away from me — I was most concerned watching this bird in the car — and anyway, it 'ud only have made things more complicated if I'd shot 'em, you know.'

The ex-wrestler scratched his head. 'Mebbe so. I wouldn't know, really.' He bent to stare into Brenda's car. 'Who was they, anyroad? They did 'elp you to get away, di'n't they?'

'They did — while you were fast asleep. But we hadn't much time for conversation, and I didn't ask them who they were. Two local girls, probably. No doubt they'll be heading for the nearest phone now to ring the police.' Privately, that was the last thing she expected the girls to do. They were avoiding the law, though they had done what they could to help her.

They had no idea, because she hadn't had a chance to tell them, why these people were using the derelict farm. They'd guess it was for some illegitimate purpose, but that wasn't their business, for they were on the run themselves.

Buster straightened up and spoke to the other man anxiously.

'Say, Kit, looks like both of us is in a spot o' trouble when the missus gets back. Me for dozing off on the job — but I couldn't help it, really — and you for letting them young dolls get away. I see how one of 'em took you by surprise, like, with that there stone. You oughta have — '

'Can it,' Kit said. 'What puzzles me is, where's Smedley? Wasn't he supposed to keep a lookout round the buildings? Why didn't he see this bird and those other two making a break?'

Brenda put her head out of the side window.

'Smedley's been knocked out, by one those young dolls you mentioned. You're not a very efficient lot, are you?'

The man Kit who seemed, intellectually, to be several O-levels above Buster, made a sudden decision.

'Into the car, mate, back seat. I'll sit alongside her. We'll go back up to the farm.'

He moved quickly, and so did Buster. Kit pitched his rifle on to the rear seat, Buster jerked off the loudly-patterned tie he wore. Before Brenda could avoid it, the tie was round her neck, lightly, but firmly. Behind her, Buster growled, 'It won't get any tighter if you act proper, lady.'

There was nothing for Brenda to do but to reverse the car and drive back to the farm. She was both downcast and apprehensive — she should have remembered, when she had first been driven here, that she had heard some conversation at the gate, she might have guessed this gang would place a guard there.

As she drove, under orders, into the barn, a very sick-looking little man came weaving out of the stable. Smedley was on his feet, if only just. He was clasping the back of his head tenderly, but the other two men had no time for him just then. Helpless in their combined grasp, Brenda was hustled up the stairs and flung down upon the old bed once more.

'Have to tie her up again,' Buster grunted. 'Only thing is, I got no cord. What's more, some bastard has pinched me knife.'

Brenda managed a small secret grin. Typical Elsie Thompson! Buster wasn't likely to see his knife again — ever.

'Well, you'll have to find something,' Kit argued. 'So — half a minute, though.' He picked up one of Brenda's cut bonds. 'Unless you use something exactly the same as this, Chuck or the boss'll be sure to notice, and then . . . Here, outside a minute.'

They went out on to the landing, and a muttered discussion began there. Brenda jumped up from the bed and moved quickly to the window. But the view it gave was only that of the track to the gate and the road, beyond which a high hedge cut off any sight of the surrounding countryside. As a means of identifying where this place was, it was hopeless. She went back to the bed, paused to take a couple of large sandwiches from the open packet, still on the floor by the chair. Her watch said it was half-past two, and, normally a hearty eater, she was missing her lunch. She sat on the bed while the muttering continued.

One of the men went downstairs and she heard voices in the kitchen before he returned to the landing. She had finished her second sandwich before the two men came back into the room. It was clear they had come to some decision. It was also clear that the man Kit was to be the mouthpiece.

'Look, miss,' he began. 'You've got to stay here, as you very well know, till Mrs Ban — Mrs Lingford comes back. Now, we could tie you to that bed again, and that wouldn't be comfortable, eh? So as long as you behave yourself — and you won't get away again — believe me — we'll let you stay loose, on one condition. That you don't mention Buster here went to sleep on his job or that I didn't manage to stop those two girls at the gate.'

Brenda considered the proposition. 'I'm willing to agree,' she said, 'but I can't see it's going to do you much good. When the girls ring the police, and the patrol cars arrive, all will have to come out, you know.'

Kit grinned, completely unperturbed. 'Those two won't sing. I don't know who they were, but I've had a talk to Smedley, who's practically normal now, except for a lump on his thick skull, and from what he saw of them, it's quite clear they were hiding out here. And they looked to me like a couple on the run, I mean, the state of their clothes, their hands, their hair. They'd been living rough, and that sort doesn't call copper.'

Brenda shrugged. Another bluff which hadn't come off, and how completely she agreed with him about Elsie and Jean!

'All right,' she said, 'I'll play along. I could do with something to drink, though. I don't like beer, so what about some water?'

'Bin cut off long ago,' Buster told her. 'There ain't a drop of drinking water on the place. It's beer or nothing, miss.'

'Mrs Lingford has a spirit stove,' Kit said. 'Makes tea on it. But that's kept in the Vauxhall, along with a water canister, while we've been using this place. You'll have to wait till she comes back. You might be able to screw a cuppa out of her.'

'I'll live in hope, then.' Brenda leaned back against the wall. 'You're a dirty set of crooks, aren't you? The racket you're on is worse than murder.'

She saw anger flare in Kit's eyes. 'We obey orders and draw our pay,' he grunted. He took the rest of the sandwiches and a couple of bottles of beer from the crate. 'I'll fix Smedley up with some of this, then I'll get back to my job,' he told Buster over his shoulder and went away down the stairs.

Buster, clearly uncomfortable now at being left alone with his charge, began to pace the room. After some half-minute of this, Brenda lost patience.

'Oh, for goodness sake, Buster,' she pleaded. 'Sit down in that chair and relax. I've promised I won't give trouble. I mean it.'

Buster slumped down as directed, sighing heavily. Brenda said, 'How much longer does this go on?' He shook his head sadly.

'Search me, miss! Till them two come back, I s'pose. Might be hours yet.'

'You haven't got a pack of cards on you? Or a snakes and ladders board? Just to make time pass?'

He grinned sourly in reply.

'Then how about telling me the story of your life, Buster?'

'You wouldn't be int'rested, miss.'

'In that case, let me tell you what happened to a gang of drug-pushers the Metropolitan Police cleaned up recently. You may not have seen it in the papers. You'd think only the principals would have got heavy sentences, and the people who were just paid to work for them would have got off lightly. Instead — '

Buster waved his huge hands at her like a bear pawing at a swarm of bees.

'I know naught about drugs and drug-pushers, so willya stop riding me, miss? I don't see why I gotta take it from you. Any more, and I'll call Smedley up here and we'll tie you down again and this time I'll tape yer mouth, I will!'

He meant it, too. Brenda saw that. She leaned back against the wall again and for half an hour or more they sat in uneasy silence. Brenda was puzzled about Buster's professed ignorance of the drug racket. Surely he'd been told the game he was on? Or was he just being employed as a muscle man, kept outside the gang's confidence? She was pondering this when, at the sound of an approaching car, Buster jumped up and went to the window. He let out an explosive gust of relief.

'That's them back now, thank Gord!' He swung to face Brenda. 'You'll remember what you promised, now?'

'Don't worry,' Brenda told him. She was relieved also. At least, something was likely to happen, good or ill.

She heard the voices of Chuck and the woman below and then Mrs Lingford ran lightly up the stairs and came into the room. Her first glance was towards Brenda. She frowned.

'Why isn't she still tied up?' she demanded of Buster.

'Ah, well, ma'am, you see, she went sorta numb, them cords was playing 'ell with her circulation. Almost passing out, she was. She said she'd give me no trouble if I'd loose her, so I cut her free and she hasn't.'

Mrs Lingford's face cleared. She seemed to be in quite good humour.

'You did right, my man. We don't want her harmed, do we?' She nodded at the remainder of the sandwiches and the beer. 'Has she had anything to eat or drink?'

'Just a couple of sam'wiches, that's all. Said she didn't like beer. Asked if she could have a cup of tea.'

'I'll see to that.' She went downstairs again. There was another long wait and Brenda wondered what the next move of the gang would be. She herself was an obvious liability to them. There was a way by which liabilities could be cancelled out, but she didn't care to dwell on that. She concentrated on trying to remember the exact inflections of Mrs Lingford's voice when she had said, 'We don't want her harmed.' She could recall no sarcasm, no underlying threat in the words.

There was the rattle of crockery on the

stairs and the woman re-entered, a cup and saucer in each hand. She took one to Brenda, presenting it with quite a friendly smile. Then she went to stand by the window, sipping from the other cup.

Brenda drank gratefully. The tea was well-made and cool enough to swallow quickly. She hadn't realized how desperately thirsty she had become. She finished the cup, put it on the floor by her feet.

Once again she leaned back against the wall. The afternoon sun had moved round, so that it didn't shine into the room now. But all the same, it was exceedingly close in there. Brenda's eyelids were becoming very heavy. She tried to jerk them open, but they fell again like leaden weights. As she slipped sideways, the last thought in her drowsy mind was the realization that she had been given a very powerful Mickey Finn indeed.

★ ★ ★

She woke, conscious of darkness and cold. She was sitting slumped behind the wheel of a car. She rubbed her face with her hands, forcing herself to throw off the effects of the drug which had knocked her out. Her head, her limbs, seemed reluctant to return to life. With an effort, she opened the car door and stumbled out, drawing in deep gulps of cool air.

She was standing in a field, wet with heavy dew. As her brain cleared, she made out the bulk of a hedge in front of her, and a gate a few yards away. She recognized the car as her own; it was too dark to see the time on her wrist-watch, so she got into the Triumph again and switched on the roof light. Ten minutes past eleven, she had been out between seven and eight hours.

Her handbag was on the seat beside her, she checked through it, everything was in place. She sat and thought for a few moments. She wanted to get herself home, yet, should she touch the steering wheel, the gear lever? There might be prints there she ought to preserve. Hardly likely, though, this gang seemed well-organized, they wouldn't miss a point like that. She decided to risk it.

She stepped out of the car again, crossed the grass to the gate. Beyond it was a secondary road, almost a lane. It didn't even rate a white line along its middle.

Brenda hadn't the faintest notion where she was. She opened the gate, drove the car through it, closed the gate. Now, right or left? It was an even-money bet. And then, some half mile away on her right, she saw the headlights of a travelling car. It was soon followed by another, and another. With this indication of a major road, her choice was made for her. She set her car in motion.

There was a three-armed signpost at the end of the lane. Pointing back in the direction from which she had come, one arm announced 'Brandsfield 2,' the others, set side by side, said, 'Deniston 12,' and 'York 15.' When she had taken the left-hand turn for home, she glanced at her petrol gauge. It told her, most decisively, that her car had done quite a journey that day. She had been taken south of Deniston, of this she was sure, but now here she was to the east of it.

At a quarter to twelve she ran the car into the garage at her home and sat for some time, wondering what she ought to do next. Get in touch with authority, she supposed, but if she rang Kingsmead House, her headquarters, she'd only get the night-duty officer, and he couldn't do much with the vague story she would have to tell. Even if the deserted farm could be found, the gang wouldn't be there now. Mrs Lingford had said they were clearing out.

Brenda had had a long and exhausting day. She was still feeling some of the effects of the drug; she had had to concentrate hard to keep her senses about her as she drove home. What she needed most now was food, a hot bath and then more sleep. Surely, an official report could wait until morning?

Having decided that it could, she locked the garage and let herself into the house. Her mother, hearing her moving about, called out to her from upstairs. Brenda said she was all right, that she'd rustle up some food for herself, that she was going to have a bath. She ate and drank, went wearily upstairs. The bath did nothing to ease her overwhelming sleepiness. She made as quick a job of it as she could, and she was dead to the world almost before her head touched the pillow.

8

She was awakened by her mother shaking her shoulder. Brenda struggled to sit up, to take the cup of tea her mother had brought.

'It's just on half-past eight,' Mrs Sheldon said. 'I thought I'd let you sleep on, as you came in late. I got that message yesterday to say you'd been called in from leave for some special job or other. I'm just off to the shop. Oh, and Inspector Joynton and that sergeant of his have turned up. He wants to see you. I told him he'd have to wait till I made you a drink and you got dressed.'

'Mr Joynton?' Brenda was still not fully awake, though she remembered the fake call Chuck had made to her mother the previous morning. 'What's it all about?'

'He wouldn't say. But he seems a bit impatient, dear, so you'd better hurry up. Oh, and I've rung the hospital. Gertrude's improving marvellously now. And you'll get your own breakfast, won't you?'

Brenda said she would and forced herself out of bed. She showered and dressed quickly, drinking her tea as it cooled. It was no use speculating on the subject of this visit from Joynton — probably something to do with the business of Mrs Avery. She ran downstairs into the lounge.

'Good morning, sir! Good morning, Sergeant!' she greeted. 'Sorry to have kept you waiting, but this is rather an early call.'

Joynton, lath-like, grizzled, with cold grey eyes in a lean face, unfolded his long form from the easy chair he had taken, while the ginger-haired Swayne, who had been staring out of the window, gave Brenda a brief grin in which sympathy was mixed with apprehension.

'We are investigating an incident which took place last night in Belsize Avenue, Deniston 16, Miss Sheldon,' Joynton said. His voice, as ever, was harsh, and came through thin lips which hardly moved. 'A young man, Arnold Toller, was stabbed to death.' He was watching Brenda closely and saw the sudden widening of her eyes. 'I believe the name is known to you?'

'I've heard it,' Brenda answered slowly. She was fighting a sense of shock. 'but I've never met Arnold Toller, Inspector.'

'How, then, did you come to know his name? Did you know his address as well?'

'Yes . . . But it's rather a long and involved story.'

'Which I shall have to ask you to tell me. In detail, too.'

'Shall we all sit down?' Brenda suggested. She was needing her breakfast but, regretfully, she knew that would have to wait.

As the two men complied, the normally cheerful Swayne said solemnly, 'With respect, sir, I think we should first tell Miss Sheldon that — '

Joynton swung round on him. 'You will allow me to conduct this interview in my own way, Sergeant. I'll ask for guidance from you when I need it.'

'Very good, sir.' Swayne subsided, but he still seemed unhappy. Joynton looked at Brenda. 'Well, Miss Sheldon?'

'It was like this.' As briefly as she could,

Brenda told how she had spoken to Karen Harkness about the young man who had tried to make her acquaintance outside Mrs Avery's shop, and how Karen had given her the name of The Groove Cafe, which the youth said he frequented.

'I went there hoping to see this young fellow,' she said. 'Miss Harkness had described a certain birthmark on his face, which would have identified him. I didn't see anyone there who fitted his description, but by chance I got into conversation with another lad, who had met Toller, and who gave me his name and address. That, I think answers your question, sir.'

'You suspected he was the person who attacked Mrs Avery?'

'I had reason to believe he might be, sir.'

'And in this business you were working on your own, unofficially?'

'Well, yes, sir. I'm on leave at present, and Mrs Avery is a close personal friend, as you know.' She added hastily, 'Had I found the slightest piece of information which would have been of use to you, sir,

I'd have handed it on at once, of course.'

'You were especially keen to see Mrs Avery's attacker brought to justice, I take it?'

'I'm in the Force, sir. Like yourself and every member — '

Joynton broke in on her. 'But here you had a personal motive, which might cause you to be possessed by a strong desire for revenge?' His hand was raised suddenly. 'No, please don't answer that now.' He gave a dry cough and continued on a fresh tack. 'Last night Mrs Avery was well enough to talk. She gave one of my officers an excellent description of the youth who attacked her. Though he was wearing a stocking mask, it had been pulled on in a hurry. She saw this birthmark. She had noticed it on a previous occasion when the same youth — she is positive he was the same — came into her shop and chatted her up, mainly asking her if she ran the place on her own, at what times was she busiest, and so on. In my mind it's certain that Toller was the person who spoke to her then and who attacked her on

Monday last.' He paused, rubbing his narrow jaw with long fingers. 'Miss Sheldon, I find myself in an awkward position. I feel this is the moment when I should give you the usual caution.'

Brenda's eyes widened. She started forward in her chair.

'Caution? What on earth are you talking about, Mr Joynton?'

'Miss Sheldon, I believe you own a dark-blue car, a Triumph?' Some of the normal harshness had gone from his voice now, and at Brenda's nod he continued, 'Give me its registration, please.' He took a notebook from his pocket.

Brenda told him, he glanced at an open page and nodded glumly.

'Toller was knifed outside his home in Belsize Avenue. We have a witness, a man named Kane. He was walking along the Avenue, Toller was coming towards him. Kane said they were still some eighty yards apart when a car pulled up, a man got out, stabbed Toller twice, ducked into the car again. The car approached Kane as he ran forward to help Toller. A woman was driving it, he couldn't see her clearly, nor the man who did the stabbing. But he got the car's number, we checked in the usual way — there was some delay about this, but the details don't matter — and we found you were the owner, Miss Sheldon. By that time it was early this morning, we've not had a chance to see you until now. But' — his voice had become hard again — 'you'll realize I must ask you for an account of your movements last night.'

Brenda considered quickly. She had believed, having stumbled on what she now knew was a drug racket, that Hallam at Regional should have the details before anyone else. But circumstances had changed now. It was clear Joynton considered her as a prime suspect in Toller's killing; she must clear herself at once.

'It could have been my car,' she said. 'Let's say it certainly was. But I wasn't driving it. At nine-thirty last night I was — Well, I don't know where I was, but wherever I may have been at that time, I was deeply asleep, under the influence of some very strong drug.'

Joynton frowned at her. 'You'd better give me the facts.' And his tone underlined the last word. He gestured at Swayne, who took out a notebook and pencil.

Brenda began her story with her encounter with Dave Morgan's boys, she told of her conversation with Dave at the Duncan Street gym, of the fake telephone message the following morning, of her capture and her forced journey to the farm. She related her escape, her recapture, her wakening in her car, her journey home the previous night. Swayne's pencil galloped in shorthand over the pages of his notebook. And, when she had finished, Joynton, who had sat unmoving throughout the recital, let out his breath in a gusty sigh.

'You're prepared to sign a statement that all these things happened' he asked. 'It all sounds very much like a fairy tale, you know.'

'But it's true,' Brenda protested. 'Unfortunately, I've no definite idea where this derelict farm is, though it's somewhere just ahead of one of the new motorways.' She got up, crossed to a bookcase and took out a large-scale map of the Deniston area. Swayne came forward to help her to spread it on the lounge table. Brenda's fingers hovered over the map, then came down on it.

'Here's the minor road I came along, out of the field. It joins the main road here.'

Joynton had also risen, and was peering over her shoulder. 'That might give us a start,' he said doubtfully. 'You realize, don't you, that this story of yours has to be proved — up to the hilt?' Brenda nodded gloomily.

'So,' Joynton went on, 'We'll start by examining your car.'

Brenda picked up her handbag from the small table where she had left it the previous evening. Joynton said, 'Handle it carefully. That shiny surface might carry some good dabs.' Brenda opened the bag, took out her keys and the membership card of the St Faith's Youth Recreation Centre which Johnny Pitts had given her. 'Here's one piece of evidence to support part of my story,' she said drily. 'And now, sir, I'd like to ring Mr Hallam at Regional. I think he should know about the trouble I seem to be in.'

Joynton considered a moment. 'Toller's killing is under my jurisdiction, of course. But if, as you think, there's a drug angle to this business, that's a pigeon for Regional. And I'll let you report it, Miss Sheldon. If I may use your telephone first. I'd like to get my fingerprint men here.'

Brenda said, 'You're welcome, of course.' She went into the kitchen, where her mother had left her usual cornflakes, and bacon and eggs, ready for her. As she lit the gas stove, the inspector's voice called to her.

'The phone's free now, Miss Sheldon. And I've no doubt Mr Hallam is in his office by this time.'

'Thanks,' Brenda called back, 'but I'll do that when I've had something to eat.'

'You will oblige me by doing it now.' Joynton had come into the kitchen, the severe look was again on his face. 'And I feel it's my duty to listen to your end of the conversation.'

Brenda's lips tightened. 'So I'm still

suspected, am I? Very good, sir, you can listen all you want.'

She strode past him into the hall. 'Brenda Sheldon here, Judith,' she said to the switchboard operator at Kingsmead House. 'I'd like to speak to Mr Hallam if he's available.'

'Hang on, love.' There was a pause and then Hallam's voice announcing himself. Brenda took a deep breath.

'I'm in terrible trouble, sir,' she said rapidly. 'A youth named Arnold Toller of Belsize Avenue was stabbed to death last night. Detective-Inspector Joynton, who is here with me now — I'm ringing from home — tells me he has reason to think I could know something about this killing. I don't, of course, but my car was used for the job. It's a long and involved story, which I won't bother you with now, the main point being that I believe I have uncovered an organization which sells and distributes drugs. I feel you should know about this. Inspector Joynton agrees.'

There was a pause. Brenda could imagine her chief with the receiver still at his ear, his grey eyes misted with concentrated thought. Then he spoke.

'We'll have to do what we can for you, Brenda.' She could detect neither doubt nor reproach in his voice. 'Ask Mr Joynton if he'll talk to me now, will you?'

'Yes, sir.' Brenda held out the receiver. As Joynton took it, she went back into the kitchen.

She was finishing her cornflakes, and the eggs and bacon were sizzling in the pan, when the inspector came in. His expression now, she noted, was definitely more friendly.

'I've asked Mr Hallam for assistance in this business, at any rate with the drug angle you say you have turned up, Miss Sheldon,' he said. 'He is sending a man down here. You will, of course, remain here for the present.'

Brenda nodded, he went away and she continued with her breakfast. Though she had little to support what she knew must sound a fantastic story, she wasn't unduly worried. Joynton was a man who stuck rigidly to the book, and he would have cautioned her formally had he had any serious suspicions of her. If he put any credence at all in what she had told him, he would have already realized that her car could have been used for the business of stabbing young Toller, and she felt convinced the man who was called Chuck was responsible for that. Also, she would have laid heavy odds that the woman who had been seen with the killer was Mrs Lingford.

She finished her meal, cleared away and washed up. From the kitchen she could see Joynton and his men busy in and around her car. They had pushed it out on to the drive, it was being extensively dusted for prints. She didn't think they would find any except her own.

She was putting the last plate away when another car drew up outside and the tall, trim figure of her colleague, Detective-Sergeant Richard Garrett, strode up the drive. Brenda watched him talking to Joynton for some time. Then Garrett came to the back door. Brenda went to answer his knock. He grinned at her.

'Well, you are a bright beauty,' he

greeted her. 'From what I hear, you turn yourself into a private eye and then jump into trouble with both feet. Mr Joynton has given me the main facts, but we'll be going over them again at H.Q. — Mr Hallam's instructions. But first we'll take a ride in my car and look for that field you found yourself in last night. Trevor Swayne is coming with us. How long will it take you to get ready?'

'Five minutes, Dick, no more.'

'I'll allow you three. We've lots to do this morning.'

Brenda rushed upstairs, dabbed on some make-up and was locking the house behind her in four minutes flat. Swayne winked at her as he got into the back seat of Garrett's car.

'I'm merely going along to see that you and this bloke don't make a break for one of the channel ports, or some handy airfield,' he said. 'Actually, it'll be a relief to be free of the Old Man for a while. He's always at his most trying at the start of a case. No helpful dabs on your car, by the way, Brenda.'

Directed by Brenda, Garrett made

good time through the city and so to its eastern outskirts. Twenty minutes from starting, he was turning his car right-handed by the triple-armed signpost into the minor road Brenda had used the previous night. Beside him, Brenda leaned forward as he moved slowly along the road.

'That's it!' she said suddenly. 'That gate, just ahead on the left. The top bar of it is hanging loose, I caught my hand on it when I was opening the gate last light.'

Garrett drew up, they all got out. Brenda was hastening forward to the gate, but Garrett laid a restraining hand on her arm.

'We'll let Trevor go first,' he said. 'Then we can't be accused of faking evidence on your behalf.'

Swayne turned on him, glaring. 'I'd never — ' He saw the grin on Garrett's face and his own lightened in a smile. 'One of these days I'll learn to know when my leg's being pulled!'

But all the same, he went ahead, opening the gate just enough to squeeze through. The other two stayed on the road, watching Swayne while he cast to and fro like a questing hound. After a couple of minutes he beckoned them to join him.

'No problem here,' he said, and there was relief in his voice. 'Look, you can see where a car's been driven in recently, and out again. Like the little lad said, they always put a gate in the muddiest part of the field, and those tracks fit the tyres on your Triumph, Brenda. There's a footprint in the mud which I reckon is yours, too.' He looked at her shoes and nodded. 'No other prints, though, but whoever brought you here and left you was probably careful about that. What's more, you drove through a cowpat, look, and there are traces of manure in the treads of one of your tyres. As far as I can judge, your car was driven in up to this point here. You agree, Dick?'

Garrett nodded. 'Driven in, turned to face the gate and left just here. What are you looking for, Brenda?'

She had come forward and was bending down, staring at the grass.

'There's a slight oil leak in my car,' she

said. 'I was wondering if we could find some traces of it, they'd tell us how long the car stood here.'

They all searched carefully without result. 'Negative evidence,' Swayne commented, 'which seems to say you weren't here very long. Wait, now, while I work it out. Toller was killed at nine-thirty, you say you woke up here at ten past eleven, Brenda. One hour and forty minutes. That would give ample time for the car to be driven from the scene of the crime to here. Whether you were in the car when Toller was stabbed can't be proved, I suppose.'

'At any rate, I wasn't driving it!'

'I don't say you were, love. But they could have dumped you on the floor at the back — we'll have to see the clothes you wore last night — dustmarks and so on — or they may have picked you up somewhere after they'd done Toller. By the way, we found a couple of blood spots on the floor by the front seat. Probably from the killer's knife. Messy way, stabbing. Me, I'd always strangle 'em. Ah, well, let's get back.'

9

They were sitting in Hallam's office, the Chief Superintendent himself, Chief Inspector 'Jack' Spratt, who, tall, lean, lantern-jawed, might have been Hallam's twin, Sergeants Garrett and Norwood and Brenda Sheldon. She had just told her story once again, in full detail, as Hallam had ordered. He had leaned back in his chair during the recital, his eyes turned to the ceiling, smoke from his pipe rising in regular puffs. She knew he was storing the facts in a memory which never let him down. Spratt, notebook on knee, scribbled an occasional word or two, while Garrett sat and watched her face. Detective-Sergeant Barry Norwood, recently promoted from detective-constable, put down every word she said in shorthand, as was his conscientious custom.

'So,' Hallam said when Brenda had finished, 'you see what can happen when a police officer decides to go it alone, despite a warning as to the inadvisibility of so doing. He — in this case, she — can land into very serious trouble.' He leant forward, placed his pipe on the desk ashtray. 'Now, having administered the necessary official rebuke, we'll see what we can do to get you out of the spot you're in, Brenda. You didn't have anything to do with Arnold Toller's killing — right. We believe you, but working on the motive angle alone, Counsel could make an excellent case against you, don't you agree, Mr Spratt?'

'I do. But you'll agree, too, sir, that it isn't only a matter of throwing doubt on a prosecutor's argument. Because she is a member of the Force, we'll have to see to it that Brenda is shown to be completely and entirely clear of the whole thing; in fact, that she doesn't have to appear in Court at all under any sort of charge.'

'Honestly, sir,' Brenda expostulated, 'I'd nothing to do — '

Spratt cut her off. 'We know that. But you did want to see Toller brought to justice and suitably punished for what he did to your old friend. Inspector Joynton is aware of this. He's bound to work on that lead, at least, until he finds another.'

'So,' Brenda said with more than a touch of bitterness, 'I get some information which Inspector Joynton missed because of his unfortunate manner with a person he interviewed, I follow it up and uncover an organization running drugs, and as a result I find myself practically on a murder charge. And, of course, it seems I was able to put my hand at once on a killer who'd do the job for me. And there's another thing. I did all this after I knew Mrs Avery was going to get better, which makes me out as — '

She broke off, suddenly conscious of the four grinning males who were facing her.

'All right,' Hallam said. 'You've got it off your chest, so let's get down to brass tacks. Proving the truth of your story is important, since if there is a drug-running gang here, we've got to lay them low. That is first priority. Now, I've talked to Mr Joynton and we've agreed on a plan. He will continue his investigations into

Toller's death. It's necessary, too, to find those absconding girls, Thompson and Hathorn. An all-stations call went out, of course, when they were reported missing from Westwood, and they're bound to be run to earth sooner or later. Meanwhile, our job here at Regional is two-fold. There's the drug angle, with The Groove Cafe as a possible lead. Norwood, I'm giving you that job. You can also talk to Dave Morgan and as many of his lads who may seem able to help you. Garrett, you're going to try to find the farm where Brenda was held captive. You will take her with you. Any questions?'

'Yes, sir.' This from Norwood. 'I'd like Miss Sheldon to give me a detailed description of all the people, excepting the girls, of course, who she saw at that farm.'

'Mr Spratt and I dealt with that before we called you and Garrett in here, Norwood. There's a general alert out for them now. But Mr Spratt will let you have the details, all the same. That seems to be all, then. And the sooner you start, the sooner you'll finish.'

Spratt added, as the three went out, 'You'll find those descriptions on my desk, Norwood. Help yourself. And now, sir' — he turned to Hallam as the door closed — 'about that enquiry from Manchester which came in this morning. I think we should deal with it straight away, don't you?'

Hallam nodded, and then the intercom on his desk buzzed at him. He pressed a key. 'Yes?'

'There's a gentleman here, sir,' his secretary replied, 'who insists on seeing you. A Mr Robert Toller. Councillor Toller.'

Hallam raised his eyebrows at Spratt. 'Show him in, please,' he said and then, as he broke the connection, 'Arnold Toller's father. He's on the City Council, Labour ward. You stay put, Jack. This might be sticky.'

The man who came in was big, heavily-made, with a round red face and a thick greying moustache. He pushed past the secretary and strode into the office like a man who knew what he wanted and was going to make sure he got it.

Hallam rose, put out a hand. The visitor didn't seem to see it. He spoke in a high, light voice which was at odds with his bulk.

'I am Councillor Toller. You'll have heard of me.'

A blusterer, Hallam thought, and extremely short on manners. However, in the circumstances, the man must be excused.

'Sit down, sir.' He indicated the chair Spratt was placing on the other side of the desk. 'We have met once, briefly. You serve on the Deniston Watch Committee, of course.'

'Don't remember you. It is Hallam, isn't it? And who's this fellow?'

'Chief Inspector Spratt, my second-in-command here. I know he joins me, sir, in offering you sympathy. You have suffered a grievous loss.'

Toller's thin lips tightened under his heavy moustache.

'That's why I'm here, Hallam. My son — my only child — has been foully done to death. I'm demanding the utmost efforts of you people to bring his

147

murderer to justice.'

'Detective-Inspector Joynton is in charge of the case, sir. He and his staff are working all out on it. I can assure you — '

'Joynton! I know him. In my view, he's not competent enough for a matter of this sort. You're supposed to be more efficient here at Regional. I want you and your men on the case, every one of you!'

Despite his understanding of a father's feelings, Hallam wasn't to be dictated to like this. He kept his tone level.

'You are mistaken in your assessment of Inspector Joynton's capabilities, sir. And you should be aware that Divisional matters are dealt with by the Division concerned. Normally, we don't interfere, we co-operate only when we're asked to do so. Inspector Joynton has already sought our assistance. Three of my officers are at work now on lines which, though incidental to your son's death, should eventually lead to the apprehension of the man who killed him. I assure you, everything possible is already being done.'

'I'm extremely glad to know that.' Some of the aggressiveness had gone now. 'You'll realize, I'm sure, how devastatingly shocked and grieved I am feeling.' It was almost an apology. Toller swallowed hard and continued. 'I gave Joynton an interview last night, after — after it happened. I was unable to help him with his enquiries as to my son's habits and friends. This crime appears to me to be entirely motiveless. A homicidal maniac is my theory.'

'Homicidal maniacs work alone, sir. This man had an accomplice, the woman who drove the car.'

'H'm. I see you know some of the facts, at least. Well, you may be right.' He heaved a deep sigh and then, almost as if he were repeating an old self-argument he went on, his high voice muted.

'His mother died when he was ten. But I've given him everything, everything. I've always been a busy man, managing director of my firm and with my local political work, too. Maybe I left the boy alone too much.' His shoulders lifted and fell, then he broke out again angrily.

'What has come over the youth of today? Why can't we, the older generation, get anywhere near to them? God knows, I made the effort with Arnold, yet we were almost strangers. Joynton's theory is that he was mixed up in some sort of dirty business. How could this have come about? Why didn't he confide in me?' They saw him make an effort to control himself, saw him succeed. Abruptly, he got up.

'I hope I haven't wasted too much of your time, gentlemen. I came because I believe in contacting men at the top. It's a business maxim of mine.' He hesitated, as if he would say more, then turned away. 'I'll wish you both good-day.'

Spratt saw him out. When he returned to Hallam's office the chief inspector said, 'I wondered if you'd mention drugs to him, sir. Probably not wise at this stage?'

Hallam grinned sourly. 'That, and the attack on Mrs Avery, is Bob Joynton's job. And, Jack, I wish him joy of it!'

10

Detective-Sergeant Barry Norwood left Kingsmead House equipped with the descriptions of the people who had kidnapped Brenda Sheldon stored in his notebook and in his head. He had an excellent visual imagination and didn't think he'd have to refer to his written notes. But he took them along with him, just in case.

The Groove Cafe, he found, did a very scanty daytime trade in teas, coffees and snack lunches. It was just after twelve o'clock, but there were only nine customers — three young couples drinking coffee, a pair of middle-aged women, with loaded shopping bags on the floor by their chairs, who were indulging in baked beans on toast, and a girl sitting by herself. There was no sign of the sour proprietor Brenda had mentioned, but the long-haired assistant was there, behind the service bar, unoccupied at the moment and looking extremely bored. He jerked into life as Norwood walked up to the counter and held out his warrant card.

'Oh,' he said. 'Police. What — er — I mean — ?'

'I'd like a word with the proprietor. Is he around?'

'As a matter of fact, he's just gone across the road for a quick one.' The young man turned to glance at a wall clock. 'I'm expecting him back any minute.'

'I'll wait for him. And I'll have a cup of coffee while I'm doing so.'

'Certainly, sir.' He fumbled the job of setting up a cup and saucer, but Norwood noticed his hands were quite steady as he poured out. And he shook his head when Norwood offered to pay.

'On the house, sir. I'm sure Mr Connor would wish it that way.' He pushed a sugar bowl forward. 'You see, in a place like this, we sometimes get the odd spot of trouble from customers, and the police have always been very good — I mean, settling things and so on.'

Norwood thanked him, stirred sugar into his coffee. 'Mr Connor is the owner of this place?'

'Yes. I'm working here till I can get a proper job. Came out of university last June, you see, quite a good degree, too. But jobs aren't easy to find, especially for arts people. Though something will turn up, no doubt.'

'Oh, sure. It always does. And what's your name?'

'Michael Repton. As I was saying — Oh, here's Mr Connor now.'

The stout, bald man came in through a rear doorway, shrugging a white jacket over his fleshy shoulders. The assistant turned to him.

'This gentleman is waiting to see you, Mr Connor. He's from the police.'

Norwood was watching the small, fat-encased eyes. He thought he saw a brief flicker of apprehension there, but it was gone at once.

'Police?' Connor repeated with a grin. 'You're not one of the local lads, are you? We do have to get 'em here sometimes.'

'Detective-Sergeant Norwood, Regional

CID. I'd like to talk to you, Mr Connor. Somewhere private. Maybe we could use the room upstairs behind the curtain yonder?'

Connor wasn't grinning now. 'And suppose I say I've no time for talk, mister? I have a business to run here, you know.'

'In that case we shall be having our little chat down at the local nick. Please yourself — I'm not worried.'

Connor glared at the assistant, goggling near by. 'Think you can manage on your own for a bit longer without bankrupting me?' He jerked his head towards the curtained doorway. 'Up there, then,' he grunted to Norwood.

The sergeant lifted the curtain and joined Connor on the other side. The fat man went wheezily up the stairs and pushed open the door on the left of the landing. Norwood followed him inside.

The table and the two chairs which Brenda had described were still there but apart from them the room was completely empty. Connor crossed to the table, eased his bulk on to it. 'Well,' he said. 'Let's have it, whatever it is.'

'This room,' Norwood returned. 'What is it used for?'

'Private parties sometimes. Though I don't do much in that line nowadays.'

'Wouldn't be much of a private party with that small table and only two chairs.'

'Got the stuff stored. Look, if you'll say what you've come for . . . '

'We're getting to it, fast. Do you ever let the room for other purposes?'

'Sometimes. Mind, I don't mean for snogging jobs, or aught like that, but now and then business people hire it.' His words quickened. 'Like earlier this week. Let it to a couple of chaps from Liverpool. Took it for two nights. Y'see, they were in some big organization — they did tell me the name but I just can't remember it — and they'd put this ad in the paper for young lads as trainees. Well, they had quite a few applied and these two fellers come to Deniston to interview these what had wrote to them. And they wanted a room for the job. So I let 'em have this one.'

That lot came out well, Norwood thought. Perhaps too well. It had a smack of rehearsal about it.

'That seems fair enough,' he said. 'Point is, on Tuesday night a young fellow came up here, was dragged into this room and beaten up.'

'I don't know nothing about that. I was busy downstairs. We did have a bit of a barney in the caff that night. I had me hands full for a while. Anyway, I rang, and two of your boys came and settled it.'

'I see. Now, would you mind describing these two men from Liverpool? As thoroughly as you can?'

Connor frowned. 'I'll have to think a minute. Didn't see much of 'em, actually . . . Now, one was tall, he seemed to be the gaffer of the two, like, because he did all the talking. T'other was smaller. Let's see, now . . . '

He cleared his throat huskily, then gave descriptions which fitted, fairly accurately, the two men Brenda had known as Chuck and Smedley. Norwood thanked him.

'We're interested in these two men, Mr Connor,' he said. 'We've reason to believe the story they told you about interviewing applicants was a cover for some other business — illegal business.'

'Look, I don't know anything about that!'

'I'm not saying you do. How did they get in touch with you in the first place? By letter?'

'No. The tall bloke came in — Saturday it would be — and he said he understood I had a room to hire and he told me all this about interviewing and I said okay and he took it for the two nights and paid me in advance, and he and his mate turned up Monday evening.'

'Were they carrying anything with them?'

'O'ny a briefcase each. Big 'uns, looked pretty full, an' all. Like as if they was stuffed out with papers.'

Norwood smiled genially. 'You're being very helpful, Mr Connor. There are just another couple of things. Do you know any of these lads who came up here for interview?'

Connor shook his head decisively. 'Not a single one of 'em. I noticed 'em keep going upstairs, like, one at a time, but they was all strangers to me.'

'They went up, stayed a while and then came down again?'

'Well, they didn't come back into the caff, if that's what you mean. Becos this big bloke asked if he could send 'em out the back way.' He jerked a thumb over his shoulder. 'There's a door off the landing there. Leads to our back stairs and out behind the caff. Bloke said he didn't want these young chaps meeting, like, so's the one who'd been in could tell the next what sort of questions they'd ask. Something like that, anyway.'

'Yes, that's the normal practice. So, when they'd sent each applicant off, one of the men would come down into the cafe and call the next one up, I suppose?'

'Likely, I'd think. But wouldn't rightly know. I was too busy, we do plenty of trade in the evenings.' He stood up. 'That the lot? I oughta be behind the counter now, you know. It's time young Mike had his lunch spell.'

Norwood nodded, turned towards the door, then swung back again.

'By the way, do you know a lad called Arnold Toller?'

'Toller?' Again Connor's brows drew together. 'Seems to ring a bell. Ah, yes. Read about it in this morning's paper. Got killed, didn't he?'

'He did. And it's possible he was a customer of yours.'

'If he was, I didn't know him. Not one of me reg'lars, he wouldn't be. I mean, there was this picture in the paper, and I didn't rec'nise it as anybody I knew.'

Norwood thanked him, received his promise that if either of the men came back he'd get in touch with the police, and left the cafe. He needed lunch himself, but something more solid than The Groove offered. Seated over a substantial meal in a restaurant a few streets away, he considered his interview with Connor.

The story the proprietor had told was, on the face of it, credible enough. He'd related it without hesitation, without any signs of shiftiness. But an experienced police officer is always suspicious of a story which comes out too glibly; even the briefest and most simple relation of facts, of answers to questions, normally fail to flow easily. Rethinking what Connor had said, and how he had said it, Norwood was reminded of a television interview, where the person being interrogated already knows what questions are going to be put to him.

There was one point on which he hadn't pressed Connor, since he didn't wish to make the man too suspicious. Any large organisation, needing a room in another city to interview job-seekers, would have applied to an hotel for the purpose, not to a third-rate cafe. Norwood wondered what Connor's reaction would have been had this been pointed out to him. He fancied the man hadn't been briefed there, otherwise he'd have been quick to provide a reason, even before one was asked for.

There were also a couple of questions which a man with nothing to hide from the law would certainly have asked. He had been told that the men who had hired his room were suspected of doing illegal business there. Connor had denied all knowledge of this, yet he hadn't asked what sort of illegal business it was. He had shown an odd lack of natural curiosity. Again, he had been told that a youth had been beaten up in that first-storey room. He had denied all knowledge of this, too, but had not asked about the victim — who he was, how badly hurt he had been — questions which, surely, the normal man would have put. Norwood, sipping his after-lunch coffee while he jotted down the main points of his talk with Connor in his notebook, was certain the man knew a great deal more than he was prepared to divulge.

So, Dave Morgan next. Norwood paid his bill and sought the parking meter where he had left his car. Before setting out from Kingsmead House he had looked up the address of Morgan's garage. Cornwall Road was on the inner edge of the residential district north of the city.

The garage was small, but smart in appearance and well-appointed. There were half-a-dozen cars in the forecourt and Norwood found a space between two of them. He went into the main workshop behind the petrol pumps and asked a mechanic, who was setting a power-jack under the front of a gleaming Bentley, where he could find Mr Morgan. The man jerked his head towards a corner of the workshop. 'Office,' he said briefly. Norwood turned towards it.

The office was small, narrow. A desk took up most of one of its longer sides and, when his tap on the door elicited a 'Come in!' Norwood found the burly, black-haired proprietor busy with paper-work. He glanced at the card his visitor held out, got up and pulled a second chair away from a wall.

'Sit down, Sergeant, now. And tell me what I can do for you.'

'You met Miss Brenda Sheldon on Tuesday night, I understand, Mr Morgan?'

Interest sparkled in Dave's eyes. 'Yes, indeed! Quite a get-together we had at my little place in Duncan Street. But you'll know all about that. She said she'd be reporting what we talked about.' He

paused, his thick eyebrows rising inter-
rogatively.

'Yesterday morning, before she could
get in touch with our headquarters, Miss
Sheldon received a phone call, purporting
to come from you. She was asked to get
in touch with you at Duncan Street
before she reported, as important new
evidence had turned up. She went to
Duncan Street, and, in your office there,
was attacked by two men, blind-folded
and taken away in a car to a derelict farm
which, at the moment, we haven't
identified. She was kept there for most of
the day, then drugged. She woke up to
find herself in her own car in a field and
made her way home from there. She's all
right, but, naturally, we want to get to the
bottom of this mystery, especially since
two of her attackers were the men who
beat up that young friend of yours at The
Groove.'

Dave had listened wide-eyed. Now he
swore softly.

'Look you, Sergeant, it wasn't me who
rang Miss Sheldon.'

'Thinking it over afterwards, she was

sure it wasn't. It was somebody imitating your voice. Somebody who, obviously, was aware of the details of the conversation you had with her in your Duncan Street office.'

'But — ' Dave stopped, frowning. 'No, it couldn't have been either of them. Not Johnny Pitts nor Ted Blake. They wouldn't do a thing like that.'

'I know, of course, about those two, and that they were present. You're sure there was nobody else around? When she left you, Miss Sheldon saw somebody crossing the yard in front of her, she wasn't near enough to give a description.'

'When I took her upstairs, look, there was one of my lads in the office. All the rest had gone home. And I sent this boy off, too. There was nobody else at all, Sergeant.'

'I'll have to see Pitts and Blake. Can you tell me where I can get in touch with them?'

'Easy, it is. Ted Blake works at Mayword, Bell and Comstocks', solicitors they are, in Moseley Street. Training for the law, Ted is. And Johnny, he's at

Reaney and Sons', that's in Falcon Street.'

'Tailors and outfitters, aren't they?'

Dave nodded. 'Look,' he repeated, I know it wouldn't be either of them.'

'So what about the other lad, who was there when you arrived?'

'Derek Noyes? Oh, no, Sergeant. Not him, either. We're a sort of little club, you know, with Ted Blake being the leader. Derek's his second-in-command. Though,' he added dubiously, 'like Ted, he has a key to the Duncan Street office.'

'It's beyond doubt that whoever rang Miss Sheldon, telling her to go to Duncan Street, must have known of your conversation with her. If it wasn't you, or any of these lads, it must have been some other person who crept up the stairs to your office there — Miss Sheldon has described the premises to me — and listened.'

The Welshman nodded again. 'That makes sense, now, as far as it goes. But who'd know she was there at all? She came straight from The Groove to

Duncan Street, after Ted Blake had rung me, suggesting this.'

'And you were alone when you took the call?'

'I was, Sergeant. All the lads had gone to The Groove. They came back to report — bar Ted and Johnny — just after Ted had rung. I listened to what they had to say and sent 'em all home.'

'All except Derek Noyes. So I'll have to see him, too.'

'He works at the same place as Johnny Pitts, Sergeant. That's how he came to join the club. Big fellow, well-made, so Johnny got him interested.'

'That makes it very convenient for me. I can see Pitts and Noyes at the same time. Now, Mr Morgan, tell me why you suspected The Groove Cafe was used for drug-pushing.'

Dave rubbed at his chin. 'You know about my son Lewis?'

'I do, and so I understand why you've a down on that filthy business.'

'That's right, now. Well, it was one evening at the club, and a few of the lads were talking and one of them, Norman

Dent, said he'd been in a caff and he'd heard these two lads at the next table talking about how you could get high, say you had the dough, if you got on the list at The Groove. I happened to overhear this so I tackled Norman about it. He just repeated what he'd told his mates, and that was all he knew. You can talk to him yourself if you like, indeed, but he won't be able to help you. Anyway, now, I thought I'd go into this and I put it to some of the lads I could trust and — well, you know the rest.'

'It would have been wiser to come to us, Mr Morgan.'

Dave shrugged. 'I discussed all that with Miss Sheldon on Tuesday night, Sergeant.'

The hint was obvious. Norwood got to his feet. 'Thank you for your time, and your help, Mr Morgan. We'll keep in touch.'

He went to his car, sitting behind the wheel for some moments while he considered his next move. He wondered if it was worthwhile interviewing the two youths, Pitts and Blake. They probably couldn't tell him any more than they had told Brenda and Morgan. But Norwood wasn't a man to miss out on possibilities. He started up his car and drove to the offices of Messrs Mayward, Bell and Comstock.

The solicitors were domiciled on the second floor of a modern office block in Moseley Street. Norwood used the stairs rather than the lift, he took his exercise where he found it. There was a door marked 'Enquiries' under the firm's name, and, pushing through it, he found a small anteroom with a counter blocking him from a teenage receptionist. She looked up, tossing her hair from her eyes to see him, then rose from her chair and came towards him, donning a professional smile.

Norwood produced his warrant card and stated his business. 'Ted Blake?' the girl repeated. 'Here, I hope he hasn't — ' She caught herself up. 'If you'll come this way, sir . . . '

She ushered him in to an empty reception room. With its leather-upholstered chairs, its central table, magazine-covered, and the air of anxious waiting it seemed to exude, it might have belonged to a doctor or a dentist. After all, Norwood reflected as he sat down with his back to a window, a solicitor was extraordinarily like a medico or a tooth-puller. One visited them only out of dire necessity.

He liked the level-eyed, handsome youth who came into the room five minutes later. 'I'm sorry to have kept you waiting, sir,' Ted Blake said. 'I was down in the vaults, where we keep our ancient and musty deeds. We rent a sort of strongroom down there. The word has flown round the general office that I am wanted by the police.' He grinned, and sat down by the table.

'I'm Detective-Sergeant Norwood, Regional Crime Squad, Mr Blake. I've no doubt you'll guess why I'm here.'

'In connection with what we told your charming colleague, Miss Sheldon, I take it? Re The Groove Cafe and its dark and dirty doings?'

'Exactly, sir. Now, I've heard Miss Sheldon's story, of course, and I've just been talking to Mr Morgan. It's possible you may not be able to add anything to their accounts but you might have noticed some detail which has occurred to you since.'

Ted hesitated this for a full minute before he shook his head.

'Sorry, I didn't. We went in there to create a mild diversion, I was in charge of the operation and I was anxious to see it didn't get out of hand. When we left, I waited outside for Johnny Pitts, met Miss Sheldon and drove to the club. That's all.'

'This is in strict confidence, of course, but had you any suspicions that the cafe proprietor knew what was going on upstairs?'

'None whatever, Sergeant. I kept an eye on him, of course, while we were in the place. His only concern seemed to be to prevent a real bust-up developing and when it looked as if it might, he rang the police at once.'

'There's one other point.' Norwood told him of the fake call Brenda had received the following morning, and why it was important, though he didn't relate the results of that call. Ted's eyebrows rose.

'From what you tell me, Sergeant, the caller must have listened in to our conversation in the club office. As I didn't ring Miss Sheldon, and Dave didn't, nor, I'm sure, did Johnny Pitts, there must have been another person, a snooper, around.' Then he frowned and said forcibly, 'But that's ridiculous! It just couldn't have been him!'

'You're referring to Derek Noyes, I think?'

'Yes, I was, but — You know he was in the office when we went up there? And that Dave sent him home? Well, look. I still don't believe Derek would do a thing like that — I mean, why should he? But there was an odd incident . . . '

'Yes, Mr Blake?'

'Johnny had been knocked about a bit. No real damage, because he's tough and he's hard. But he did need a spot of cleaning up. I took him into the washroom, put on the light. The place seemed a bit stuffy so I opened the window. Derek Noyes was in the yard below, sort of hanging about there. He must have seen the light go on, for he was looking up at the washroom window. He turned quickly away, towards the street. And, now I come to think of it, I did fancy I heard a footstep on the stairs outside Dave's office when Johnny and I went back in there and we were all talking. I was sitting nearest the door, you see.'

'Miss Sheldon spotted somebody dodging out of the yard when she was leaving. I'll have to talk to Derek Noyes.'

'Know where to find him?' When Norwood nodded, he went on, 'Still, I'm sure it wasn't him. I mean, he's never struck me as the snoopy type.'

Norwood stood up. 'I'll clear the matter up with him. Thanks for your help, Mr Blake.'

'It's been a pleasure. I'll see you out, then back to the vault again!'

Norwood found a vacant parking meter in Falcon Street, a few yards away from the outfitters' shop of Reany and Son. He was met, inside the shop, by an elderly man, impeccably dressed. The prim, meaningless smile he gave Norwood was accompanied by the formal, 'Can I help you, sir?'

Norwood introduced himself and stated his business. The smile vanished.

'Our Mr Pitts is in the fitting-room, sir, engaged with a customer. If you would be good enough to wait ... ' He indicated a chair.

'I would also like to talk to Derek Noyes, who is a member of your staff, I believe.'

'I regret, sir, our Mr Noyes is not with us today.'

'You mean he's off sick?'

'I'm afraid I do not know the cause of his absence. It seems he has just failed to — to turn up.'

'In that case I'll have to see him at his home. Can you give me his address?'

'We do not normally divulge — ' He turned with some relief as a dark-haired, slimly-built youth came forward from the rear of the shop. 'Ah, here is our Mr Pitts now.' He beckoned.

'We'll bob into the staff rest room, Mr Norwood.' Johnny Pitts suggested when

173

he had been told what it was all about. Norwood followed him into a room furnished with two armchairs, several wooden ones, a narrow table and a gas cooker. They sat down and Norwood took Johnny through his story of the preceding Tuesday evening. The lad could add nothing to what his questioner already knew.

'Right,' Norwood said then. 'Now, about your friend Derek Noyes. Did Blake tell you he'd seen him hanging about in the yard outside the club in Duncan Street?'

'He didn't. When was this?' Norwood told him, and Johnny shook his dark head ruefully.

'I was too busy just then putting cold water on my mug.' He fingered a fading bruise on his right cheek. 'And, look. I'd hardly call Derek Noyes my friend. I happen to work with him, but we've never been real close. In some ways he just isn't my cuppa. Not soul-mates, as you might say.'

'I'm told he's not here today. D'you know where he lives?'

'Stratford Avenue,' Johnny returned promptly. 'It's part of that housing estate off the Manchester Road, beyond Stratford Park. I went there once with a message from Dave. Can't remember the number, but it's about halfway down the Avenue, on the left-hand side as you come into it. He lives there with his auntie, mother's dead and he can't get on with his dad since the old man got wed again. Oh, yes, and the house is painted a horrible mauve. You can't miss it.'

The boy was right, Norwood reflected as he drove into Stratford Avenue, part of a council estate and one of the earliest the City Fathers had provided. The thin, grey-haired woman who answered his knock kept the front door on its chain and admitted grudgingly that Derek Noyes did live there. Then she corrected herself. 'That is, he used to.' She peered short-sightedly at Norwood's warrant card, sniffed doubtfully and asked him what he wanted with Derek.

Norwood didn't reply to that. 'Can you tell me where I can find him?'

She shook her head, and now she was

clearly disturbed.

'He came home from work last night,' she said, 'and he told me he was fed up with his job, and with Deniston. He said he couldn't stick it any longer and was off to find another job down south somewhere. I told him not to be a fool, but they won't listen to you nowadays, and after all I've done for him, too. He packed a bag, went off this morning. Promised he'd write as soon as he was settled.'

'Would you mind if I came in and had a look round his bedroom?'

'You got a search warrant? No? Then there's nothing doing. I mean, anybody could get hold of a card like that in your hand. Good-day to you.'

The door slammed and Norwood turned away. He knew when he was beaten.

11

'At any rate,' Garrett said, 'you're sure you turned south from Duncan Street when you set off?'

Brenda nodded. 'But that's not much help, Dick. The driver of the Vauxhall I was in took so many turns, obviously to confuse me, that I soon lost all sense of direction. The first time he stopped, we were in the country. I heard cows lowing and a tractor at work.'

'Say somewhere around here.' With his finger he circled an area on the large-scale map they were studying. 'And you say, when you got a look out of the window of this old farm, you couldn't spot any landmarks which might help?'

'No. Neither then, nor when I tried to make a break with those two girls in my own car.'

'What about the bit of countryside you did see? Did it look well-cultivated? I mean, was it still in production?'

'Yes, I caught a glimpse of a stubble field, partly ploughed after harvest, and there were sheep in another field.'

'The new motorway from the south is routed somewhere along here.' His finger moved again. 'I'm thinking on these lines. Why should a farmhouse become derelict in the middle of good farming land? Only reason I can think of is that it's in the way of some construction which will bring it down. So the farmer has to get out, find somewhere else to live, even if he can still keep his land in that area going.'

He looked up at Brenda. 'You ring the county planning people — you can use the phone in the general office — try and find the exact line of the new motorway. If you take the map with you, you can mark any line they describe. And I'll have a chat to the local N.F.U. headquarters and see if I can get anything out of them.'

Brenda said, 'Right,' and went out of Garrett's small office. He looked up a number and dialled the National Farmers' Union headquarters on his own telephone. After three different voices had promised to put him through, he talked to a jolly-sounding man who gave the impression that he would be more in place on a corn rick than in an office chair. He knew his job, however, and in a few seconds Norwood was given the name of an abandoned farmhouse, that of its previous owner, the present address of the said owner and the date when he left his former premises. He was copying the information into his notebook from the telephone scratch pad when Brenda returned with the map.

'Here,' she said as she laid it on the desk and pointed to a pencilled line. 'At the moment, the road construction has got as far as here.'

Garrett leaned forward. 'That's it! Sandshill Farm, near this village of Brandsfield. Let's go!'

They went in Garret's car. 'The N.F.U. told me,' he said, 'that the late occupant moved out last Lady Day. That's the twenty-fifth of March. So the place has been unoccupied for about seven months. Would you say that checked?'

'I would, from what I saw of it.'

'From the map it looks quite remote.

Easy to imagine this gang coming across it and deciding to use it for temporary headquarters. With luck, we'll be there in about half an hour.'

It was thirty-five minutes later when Brenda pointed excitedly. 'There we are! I recognise the gate, and the track up and — well, everything.'

She got out to open the gate where she had previously been stopped by Kit and his rifle. Garrett drove carefully along the track and into the farmyard. He got out of the car and looked about him.

'Seems quiet enough, Brenda. We'll go inside — if we can get in. That gang must have made an entry somehow.'

Brenda led the way to the door. 'Look, jemmied open,' she said, 'and then just pulled to when they left.' She stepped inside when Garrett had pushed the heavy door aside. 'Full-scale search, I suppose?'

'Hang on a minute.' They both turned at the sound of an approaching vehicle. It was a Land Rover which had seen hard service. It drew up in the yard and its driver, a burly man in a tweed suit, heavy boots and a cap, got out and came towards them. He raised the cap to Brenda, showing a thatch of white hair, and he grinned at them both, a wide grin in a weather-beaten face with a heavy white moustache on the upper lip.

'So you got here then — I take it you're police? I'm Stanley Pearson, and I used to farm here.' A large hand gripped each of theirs in greeting. 'The fellow you spoke to at N.F.U. headquarters is a relative of mine. He told me you'd been making enquiries about this place, which meant you'd some interest in it, so I thought I'd come along and muscle in.' He shrugged broad shoulders. 'Nothing much else to do nowadays, you see. I'm retired. Live in a nice modern house in Brandsfield village, which the missus thinks is the last word after forty years in this old place.' He sighed. 'I'd rather have green fields all round me still, though.' Then he chuckled richly and asked. 'What's going on, then?'

Garrett introduced Brenda and himself. 'We think the farmhouse has been used recently for illegal purposes, Mr Pearson. Possibly not for long, but during the past few days, until yesterday, say. We've some evidence the people who used it were illicitly vending drugs. They could have lit on this place and seen it as a temporary headquarters. I'm hoping you'll be able to help us to prove that theory.'

Pearson looked thoughtful. 'I s'pose it could have been done. The position is, you see, that this new road's coming right through the farmyard here. So I had to clear out, I was meaning to retire, anyway. The land's being used as long as possible, my son Charles is looking after that. But he farms out at Tannington, which is a good ten miles from here. What's left is mostly pasture, he runs a few sheep and store cattle on it. There's a bit of arable but not anywhere near the old house. So, you see, Sergeant, bar nipping across a couple of times or so every week and throwing an eye over the stock, that's all Charles sees of the place. Of course' — he grinned again, a little shyly now — 'me, I have a bit of a stroll round now and then, just for the sake of old times.'

'And when were you here last, Mr Pearson?'

'Let's see, now. Ah, it would be last Saturday morning. Everything seemed as usual then, except for this couple I happened on coming out of the barn yonder, just as I drove into the yard.'

'Could you describe them?' Brenda asked eagerly.

'Let's see, now,' Pearson repeated. And within the next minute he had produced detailed descriptions which left Brenda in no doubt at all that the pair had been Mrs Lingford and her henchman, Chuck.

'The woman told me,' Pearson continued, 'that she was interested in the architecture of farmhouses and barns. She seemed a nice woman — he didn't say much — and we got chatting. She asked all sorts of questions — did anybody live here now, and all that, and I reckon I told her the same tale as I've just told you. Here d'you think they were the ones who've been using this place for yon drug business, then?'

'We're coming to the conclusion,' Garrett replied, 'that they needed a safe and temporary headquarters from which they could do their filthy business in the Deniston district. Possibly strengthening up and extending an organisation which is already in being in these parts. If so, they're big shots in that racket. We want to get our hands on them, Mr Pearson. I suppose you didn't notice their car number — I take it they were in a car?'

'There was one on the road near the gate as I came in, and they drove off in it. But I couldn't tell you the number, nor the make. Just didn't notice. How did you rumble they were using this place, then?'

'That's a long story,' Garrett answered. 'We'd rather not go into it now.' The old farmer nodded.

'But what you do want to go into is this old house of ours, eh?' He stepped forward. 'Ah, I see how they got in, so there's no need for me to use the key I always bring with me.'

He paused, and then added, 'I reckon they took a bit of a risk. I mean, I might have turned up here again last week-end.'

'You'd probably have been stopped before you got anywhere near,' Brenda told him, and walked into the kitchen she remembered so well. Behind her, Garrett said to Pearson, 'We want to search the house, and the buildings. Some clue may have been left, though it's hardly likely. I suppose you've no objection?'

'Help yourselves. I'll give you a hand if you like. I know my way round every inch of this place.'

'Then I suggest you do the buildings, Mr Pearson, while Miss Sheldon and I go over the house. Anything unusual, that's what we're looking for.'

Pearson nodded and stumped away. 'We'll start here,' Garrett told Brenda, 'and we'll work together. Two pairs of eyes, you know.'

They found no traces at all of Mrs Lingford's gang on the ground floor or in the cellars. People can't occupy a house, even for a few days, without leaving some signs of occupation, but all these, it seemed, had been carefully removed. 'They took no chances,' Brenda commented as she mounted the stairs to the first floor ahead of Garrett. 'They're a tough, professional bunch, Dick.' She added, 'Here's the room where I was kept.'

The sagging bedstead with its load of ancient clothes and abandoned rubbish was still there. That was all. The rope ends Elsie Thompson had cut with Buster's knife had vanished, there wasn't even a trace of ash on the floor from one of Mrs Lingford's cigarettes. Garrett pulled the stuff from the bed, item by item, but found nothing. As he was putting it back, Brenda walked to the window and looked out. She saw Stanley Pearson come out of the big barn, cross the yard and disappear from sight. She was turning away when she glanced down at the windowsill, thick with dust. On it lay a small, irregularly-shaped piece of roofing tile. The dust was smudged round its edges.

Brenda prided herself on her powers of observation and her eyes had been constantly busy while she had been in this room as a prisoner. She was certain she would have noticed the piece of tile lying on the windowsill, had it been there. Now, holding it by the edges, she slid it off the sill and tilted it towards the light. There was nothing to be seen on the dark-grey, rough surface. She turned the tile over.

Printed across it were seven words in shaky capitals.

'MISS FELLER WITH GUN TRY RED LINE.'

She said, 'Come and look at this, Dick. I think it's been left here for me to find.'

Garrett walked across and took the tile from her. He repeated the words, frowning.

'Makes no sense to me. Been done, I'd say, with another scrap of tile, the old slate-and-pencil style. What's it mean?'

'I'm guessing Elsie Thompson, one of those two absconding girls, wrote it. It's that 'miss'. She has always addressed me like that. I think she found something out about the man called Kit, who stopped us getting away. But the 'try red line' has me completely foxed. The girls could have come back here to leave that message. They haven't been found yet. I checked that before we left this morning.'

Garrett shrugged. 'Let's do the rest of

the house and tackle that problem later.'

They looked into every room, poked into every hole and corner, but all to no avail. When they went downstairs again, Pearson was waiting for them in the kitchen.

'Only thing I've found out of place,' he told them, 'is that somebody's been up in the old stable loft, looked as if they'd had quite a do with themselves there, too. Courting couple, I reckon. I picked this up.' He produced a small crumpled, very grimy handkerchief. Brenda took it gingerly.

'I think I know who dropped this,' she said. 'No need to keep it, it won't tell us anything.' She flicked it into the sink, then opened her bag and took out the piece of tile. 'Have a look at this, Mr Pearson. We found it lying on a windowsill of a room upstairs. Does it mean anything to you?'

Pearson carried the tile to the kitchen window. He stood there, muttering the words over to himself.

'It's rubbish to me,' he said ' 'Miss feller' — I suppose that means fellow — 'with gun' sounds like a sort of order

to shoot at somebody and not hit 'em . . .
Nay, I can't make it out.' He came back
to them, to thrust the tile into Brenda's
hand. She looked at Garrett.

'I think we ought to give Mr Pearson all
the facts now, Dick.' And Garrett nodded
agreement.

The old farmer's eyes were wide with
astonishment long before Brenda had
come to the end of her story.

'I'll be forever damned!' he said. 'You
got tackled in with a right bunch of
villains here, didn't you, m'dear? And you
reckon one of the girls who were using
the old loft wrote that message for you to
find.' Again he repeated the printed
words. 'Would you say, when she put 'red
line' she could have meant 'red lion', only
she spelt it wrong? Because there's a pub
called the Red Lion between here and
Brandsfield.'

Brenda clapped her hands. 'I think
you've got it. Dick?'

'It's a theory, Mr Pearson. Tell us about
this pub.'

'Once, years ago, it was one of these
old coaching inns, on the roadside, a

good mile from the village. Then it sort of fell off, as it were. There's a pub in Brandsfield all us local chaps use and nobody was going to walk a mile for a pint you could get on the doorstep, like. The old Red Lion was taken over by a family who ran a small holding, and it was in that family for — oh, three generations, I reckon, according to what I've heard. Then, after the last war, when motor cars started to become more common, and this craze for driving out of the towns to have an evening drink came up, one of the brewery companies bought the old place, got its licence renewed, extended it, made it modern, a sort of roadhouse. Very posh, it is, nowadays. I've been in there a few times, though I still prefer the old Seven Bells in the village. Chap called Leslie Canfield's the land-lord of the Lion.'

'You know him well?' Garrett asked.

'I don't, and I don't want to.' Pearson grimaced. 'Too much of a loud-mouth for me. Came from down south somewhere and seems to think we're all nitwits in these parts, though he smarms round the townsfolk plenty. You think he might know something about this chap — what was his name? Kit? — who stopped you getting away from here, Miss Sheldon?'

'The two girls ran away across the field in the direction of that wood.' Brenda gestured. 'Knowing something of Elsie Thompson, I can well imagine her wanting to get her own back on Kit. I think those two lay low in the wood, and then followed Kit to the Red Lion. After which they came back here and Elsie left the message.'

'So you'll be wanting to have a word with Canfield at the Lion?'

'That seems to be the next step,' Garrett agreed. He looked at his watch. 'Half-past twelve. Do they serve lunches there?'

'They have a restaurant place, but I believe it's only open at weekends. No mid-week eating trade, you see. 'Course, you could get sandwiches and that. A snack meal, like.'

'That's what we'll do. You've been a big help, Mr Pearson. Thanks a lot. I'm sure

191

there's no need to ask you not to talk about all this.'

'I'll keep as quiet as a dead ewe,' Pearson promised. 'As for the thanks, I don't need 'em. This has made my day proper. And, look, you can't miss the Lion. Go along to the main road, turn left, and you'll see it.'

They bade him good-day, and five minutes later they drew up in the car park of an inn of screamingly-new modern construction, flat-roofed, wide-windowed, ornately porched. It glared by the wayside, tarted up and as manifestly out of place as a vicar's wife with an orange wig and false eyelashes at a Mothers' Union meeting. Its only virtue, as Garrett remarked to Brenda, was that it did not call itself Ye Olde Red Lyon.

They walked into a deeply-carpeted lounge with a shining bar running its length, well-stocked shelves backing it. The Red Lion had gone heavily rural in decoration. The lounge walls were adorned with masks of foxes, otters and hares, with Birmingham-made horse brasses and post horns, and a pair of carters' whips, in addition to a good-looking collection of sporting prints. A wagon wheel, sparkling with gloss paint, leaned in one corner, a shepherd's crook and a scythe in another. The clock above the bar was surmounted by a huntsman's velvet cap and flanked by bits, a Pelham on one side, a snaffle opposite. As Garrett said to Brenda, one didn't know whether to shout 'Gee-up!' or 'Tally-ho!' when needing service.

Apart from a couple of men who looked liked reps from agricultural seeds firms and who were drinking old and mild at a small corner table, the place was deserted. But as they moved up to the bar, a man appeared through a door to the rear of it. He was slow-moving, heavily-built, a lard-faced personage with thinning hair plastered carefully down upon a high crown. He wore an old-fashioned sleeved waistcoat with a dark-red, watered-silk pattern, his manner was pompous and he looked like a butler who had forgotten to slip on his tail coat before answering the bell.

Brenda and Garrett had each settled themselves on a high bar stool, the landlord — he had to be the landlord, Leslie Canfield — rolled himself opposite to them and wished them good morning with a dentured smile as meaningless as an idiot's grin. He asked, almost reluctantly, what their pleasure was.

Garrett said they'd like sandwiches, if possible, with a pint of bitter for himself and a shandy for his companion. Canfield inclined his head.

'Immediately, sir. Ham sandwiches? Cheese? Tongue?'

Garrett voted for ham, Brenda for cheese. These were presented to them accompanied by the half-bow of a sidesman with an offertory plate. Their drinks were placed before them with meticulous care, and, host-like, Canfield hovered, apparently ready to make conversation if they wished it.

Garrett did. 'One of your quieter times of the day?' he asked.

'We are not normally unduly busy in mid-week at this hour, sir. Later on, of course . . . ' His shoulders rose in a slight shrug.

'Modernizing the old Red Lion has been a success, then?'

'I think we may say that, sir. I have no complaints, nor has my brewery company.'

'It's awfully pretty country round here,' Brenda weighed in, responding to her sergeant's slight kick on her ankle. 'It has the makings of a real holiday centre. I expect you get guests staying here, don't you?'

'Touring couples and their families frequently honour us, madam. The inn is building up quite a reputation as an overnight stop between the south and Scotland.'

'And no doubt you'll get plenty of trade in the evenings from Deniston,' Garrett added. 'In fact, I was recently in company with a chap who couldn't speak too highly of your place here. You may know him. Middle-sized, stockily-built fellow, dark-haired, dresses a bit countrified. I didn't get his full name but his pals called him Kit.'

As they had been trained to do, both Brenda and Garrett watched Canfield's face without apparent staring. Each of them saw the wary flicker which passed across the pale blue eyes. But the plummy voice was undisturbed.

'I'm afraid I am not acquainted with your friend, sir. We get so many different people in here, as you will appreciate.'

He moved away to the far end of the bar where, with his back to them, he stood re-arranging one of the shelves for a few moments before he went through the rear door.

'Well?' Garrett asked Brenda.

'I wouldn't swear to it, Dick, but I think I spotted a reaction.'

'So did I. It might be worthwhile . . . But we'll see what Mr Hallam thinks about that. I'll say one thing for Mr Leslie Canfield, though. He puts on a very good sandwich.'

Brenda nodded. Always a hearty trencherwoman, with no weight problems, she had already cleared her plate. She turned away from the bar, then stiffened, nudging Garrett.

'Canfield's outside, in the car park,' she murmured, 'and he seems particularly interested in that load of scrap iron you drive.'

'Does he, indeed? He won't find anything there to say who we are.' He finished his beer hurriedly. 'Let's go out and catch him at it.'

But Canfield wasn't to be caught. When they got outside he was strolling round the park collecting the litter which had been blown into corners. He gave them a pale, half-apologetic smile.

'I fear we shall never educate the public into using the waste baskets we provide.' He gestured. 'You would think a person could take a mere couple of steps to deposit a cigarette carton, but no, he must throw it on the ground.'

He shrugged his shoulders, bade them good-day and watched them drive off.

'We might as well go back to Kingsmead House with what little we've got,' Garrett said, 'and the quickest way is past that farm. I can't see us getting any lead here until those two girls are found.

They're keeping well and truly out of sight this time.'

'They'll be caught — they always are,' Brenda said, and then, 'Hullo! Isn't this Mr Pearson coming along? Yes, he's signalling you to stop.'

Garrett pulled to a halt and Pearson got out of his Land Rover. A tall, loose-limbed young man, leather-jacketed, with clay-stained gumboots, followed him. Pearson grinned.

'I was hoping to catch you again,' he said. 'Get anything at the Lion, or shouldn't I ask?'

'You can ask, and the answer is no,' Garrett replied. 'Like you, we don't care for Mr Canfield much.'

'Well, look, Sergeant, I wasn't trying to do your job for you, but I remembered Frank Crosby here was tractor-ploughing one of my son's fields not far from our old farm earlier this week. I wondered if he'd seen anything. I happened to know where he was working today so I nipped over and had a word with him. Then I brought him along.'

Crosby grinned pleasantly at them. 'I

understand you're interested in any strangers who've been around here lately. Well, I reckon I saw that bloke with the sporting rifle last Monday afternoon. He was walking along towards the Red Lion, about five it was, and he had one of these canvas guncases under his arm. I was a bit curious about him, because there's no game whatsoever in these parts worth shooting at. I was just knocking off for the day and sheeting up my tackle when he walked by on the road. I saw him again when I was going home on my motor-bike. He was crossing the field just beyond the Lion and I noticed there was a little caravan in one corner of it. He was making towards this caravan.'

'Is it still there, do you know?' Garrett asked.

'No. It was there Tuesday, 'cos I looked, and again yesterday. But it was gone this morning.'

'You seem to notice things, Mr Crosby.'

'I noticed the caravan, because I've some idea of buying one of that sort.'

'Right. Who's the owner of the field?'

It was Pearson who answered. 'Gerry Makin. He's a small-holder. But you won't find him at home today. He and his missus are visiting their married daughter. Went off this morning, won't be back till over the weekend. I could get the address for you.'

'Thanks a lot, Mr Pearson.' Garrett scribbled a number on a page of his pocketbook, tore it out, handed it over. 'Would you ring me here — you have my name, haven't you? Good. Leave a message if I'm not in. Be seeing you!'

12

Detective-Inspector Joynton regarded his sergeant sourly.

'So it seems Sheldon's account of waking up in her own car and finding herself in the field could be correct, Swayne?'

'Yessir. And what's our next move?'

Joynton got up from his desk. 'We'll go and have another talk with that man' — he glanced at a sheet of paper — 'who witnessed the attack, George Kane, 17 Belsize Avenue. After that, we'll call at Toller's place. I want to see the lad's bedroom.'

Kane, an author by profession, lived in a neat detached villa which seemed to suggest his books were very succesful indeed. They found him in the garden, tidying up the borders, and when Joynton had introduced himself and his sergeant, Kane said, 'It's a lovely day. We'll talk here.'

'Very good, sir,' Joynton responded. 'Now, I've read your statement. Let's run over the main points. You were walking back home when you saw the attack?'

'Correct. It's my custom to take an evening stroll. I saw Arnold Toller walking towards me, on the same pavement I was using. I knew the lad, of course, in fact, I'd had several talks with him. A car swept into the Avenue, it stopped abruptly as it came alongside Arnold, a man sprang out, stabbed the boy twice. You have what description of the fellow I was able to give. He jumped back into the car, which then came towards me as I ran forward. I made a mental note of the car's number and make, which I put on paper at the first opportunity.

'When I reached Arnold, I saw there was nothing I could do except ring for an ambulance and the police. This I did.'

'You said a woman was driving the car, sir?'

'Yes, and since I talked to your man last night, I've recollected she was smoking a cigarrette. I saw the glow of it as the car went past me. Not a significant piece of information, I imagine.'

'It could be, sir.' Joynton was remembering Brenda Sheldon's description of the heavily-smoking woman who called herself Mrs Lingford. 'There's nothing else you've remembered?'

Kane shook his head. 'I'm sorry — and I have given the matter some concentrated thought.'

'Now, you say you were friendly with Arnold Toller?'

'Hardly that. We passed the time of day when we met, and sometimes we had a short chat.'

'Do you know anything about his friends?'

'He didn't seem to have any, around here, at any rate. He always struck me as quite the lone wolf — on a push-bike instead of the motor-cycle you'd expect at his age.'

'But I believe he was a member of a youth club?'

Kane grinned. 'That didn't last long. He told me about it. Just a lot of kids trying to butter up the vicar, was the way he put it.'

'Otherwise, quite normal, you'd say?'

Kane was frowning now. 'He was when I first knew him. But lately, say over the past two months, I noticed he'd become more jumpy, fidgetty. And he wasn't so eager to stop and talk when we met. Maybe just one of those adolescent phases, you know.'

With a glance at Joynton, Swayne put a question. 'I suppose you didn't see Arnold Toller last Monday evening, sir?'

'Monday,' Kane repeated thoughtfully. 'My agent was here all afternoon. We gave him tea in the lounge. Yes, I remember noticing Arnold pass along the Avenue on his cycle, about five-thirty, while we were at tea. I didn't see him again that day, in fact, it was the last time I set eyes on him alive, poor chap.'

Joynton looked at his watch. 'We're due for an appointment with his father, sir. Thanks very much for your help.'

At Robert Toller's house Joynton halted to let Swayne open the front gate. He stalked up the drive to the front door. On the top step he braced himself. 'I'm warning you, Swayne, we might have some difficulty here. Ring the bell, lad.'

Robert Toller answered the door. He looked them over sourly.

'I've been waiting for you. You'd better come in.'

He led the way along the hall into a small, sparsely-furnished room with a desk behind which he at once seated himself. 'Find yourselves a couple of chairs,' he grunted, and when they were seated he thrust a pointing finger forward.

'Now. You're Joynton, aren't you?' The high voice came out squeakily.

'I am Detective-Inspector Joynton, sir. This is Detective-Sergeant Swayne. I very much regret the cause of the errand which has brought us here.'

'All right, all right! Let's take that as read. I've already had it from Hallam at Kingsmead House this morning.'

Joynton's eyebrows rose. 'You were consulting Mr Hallam, sir, about the case my men and I are conducting?'

'I was, and if there's any question of protocol in your mind, you can pitch it out. I've no use for that sort of thing. I went there to demand that the best man in the city be put on the task of finding my son's killer. Hallam assured me I could rely on you, Joynton. I trust you'll prove his confidence is not mistaken.'

Joynton's eyes were narrowed and Swayne saw his chief was holding himself in with an effort. He didn't blame him.

'We have not been idle, sir,' Joynton said quietly. 'We have traced the car used by the man who killed your son. It had been stolen, of course. We also have one or two leads, admittedly slight ones at present, which we hope will enable us to find these people.'

'In that case, shouldn't you be getting on with the job, instead of sitting here talking to me?'

Again Joynton's mouth tightened and it was some moments before he replied.

'Mr Toller, I have an extremely unpleasant task before me now. Last Monday evening an elderly woman, Mrs Gertrude Avery of Heathfield, was attacked in her shop by a youth whose intention was robbery. She was seriously injured and is still in hospital. We believe the attacker was your son Arnold.'

Toller's eyes bulged as he leapt to his feet.

'But this is intolerable! It's criminally slanderous! I'll ruin you for this, Joynton. I'll — '

'You will have the goodness to sit down again and listen!' Joynton's tone whipped across the other man's protests. 'If you will think for a moment, you will realise I would not have said what I did without proof.'

The bluster went out of Toller as if he had been a pricked balloon. He looked ten years older as he lowered himself stiffly into his chair again. The high voice was a rusty whisper.

'I'll hear what you've got to say.'

Joynton had had enough of Toller for the moment. He nodded to Swayne. 'Give him the facts, sergeant.'

Swayne made a crisp job of it. He told how Arnold Toller had been seen, on a previous occasion, outside Mrs Avery's shop, how he had done his best to get information about her circumstances, how definitely the birthmark had identified him. How it was known he was away from home, on his cycle, on the evening of the attack. And that he had visited what Swayne referred to as 'a certain address' in Deniston which the police suspected of being a centre for the illegal distribution of drugs. Bunched in his chair like a half-filled sack, Councillor Toller sat with his eyes closed, a beaten man, past the stage of wincing, dumbly taking blow after heavy blow. When Swayne had finished, Toller looked, almost blindly, from the sergeant to Joynton.

'I just can't credit all this,' he muttered helplessly.

'Yes, sir, it's hard for you,' Joynton said, 'and we'd have spared you if we could. Had you any idea your son was taking drugs?'

'Absolutely none whatever.' Toller roused himself. 'See here, I can't believe you'll be able to prove whether he did or not. In which case there's no need for any such allegation to be made. Arnold's dead now. It can't help you to know if what you say is true or otherwise. And you must see, if such a theory is publicised, my own business, my political career, are likely to suffer very sorely indeed. Look, supposing you have your facts right. Supposing Arnold did attack this Mrs Avery. Well, he's paid, hasn't he? Can't you leave it at that?'

Joynton didn't reply directly. 'I've some questions to ask you, sir, and I'd appreciate straight answers. First, what money allowance did you make to your son?'

'He always had enough. He was still at school, he was to have gone to university next year.'

'Did he have a regular allowance from you?' Joynton pressed.

'Well, no. If he ran short of pocket-money he mentioned the fact to me and I gave him more, whenever he asked.'

'Did he ask frequently?'

'Once a week — something like that, I suppose.'

'Have the requests been more than normally numerous lately?'

Toller hesitated. Then, 'Now you

mention it, yes. Over the past month, I suppose. In fact, I had to have quite a severe talk to him about his apparent increased spending. He wouldn't tell me why he wanted the money. Inspector, I've always been good to the boy. I didn't begrudge him a thing . . . You're suggesting, of course, that he needed the money to buy drugs. Surely if he'd been on that game, I'd have noticed it?'

'Not necessarily, sir. At least, not until he was well and truly hooked. The police surgeon found no evidence of a hypodermic syringe having been used. But the less serious drugs are taken orally, as you know. With your permission, we'd like to search his room.'

Toller shrugged wearily. 'I suppose you'd better. This, coming on top of Arnold's death, has shattered me completely. And, even if your drug idea is correct, I still don't understand why he was killed.'

Joynton was speaking more gently now. 'We're fairly sure that quite a big drug-pushing organisation is working in the Deniston area, sir. Your son, we know, was in contact with these people. It's probable, on the evidence we have, he may have got at cross purposses with the pushers, become a potential danger to them. So he had to be — er — put out of the way.'

'That seems unlikely to me. After all, if we admit he was one of their clients — and I won't accept that yet — they had others. Why should Arnold in particular be a danger to them?'

'He had attacked Mrs Avery, sir. Clearly, with the object of getting money, though, as it proved, he was not successful there. However, had we caught up with him and he had talked to us . . . You see, sir? The gang must have known there was a risk of this. They would want to eliminate that risk.'

Toller sighed deeply. 'I suppose you could be right. If you want to see the boy's room, go right ahead. My housekeeper will show you. I must be left alone now.'

'I understand, sir. We'll make it as easy for you as we can.' Joynton and Swayne got up and went out of the room. As he closed the door quietly, the sergeant glanced back. Toller's arms were spread out on the desk, his head was bowed upon them. Swayne's former annoyance with the man had all gone now. He could only feel a most sincere pity.

13

Late that Thursday afternoon Joynton was sitting in Chief Inspector Spratt's office at Kingsmead House. As rank demanded, his chair was on the same side of the desk as Spratt's, Sergeants Garrett and Norwood, with W.D.-C. Sheldon, were seated opposite.

'Swayne and I turned over the boy's room,' Joynton was saying. 'The only unusual thing we found was a small plastic bottle containing some fifteen tablets which we've had identified as an amphetamine-barbiturate compound. In other words, the old pep pills. Relatively harmless, if it's a case of one now and then at infrequent intervals, but you know what effects regular use often has on the taker. We've talked to Toller's house-keeper, and in addition to what the author, Kane, told us, she, too, had noticed the typical agitation, the restless-ness, the depressive after-reactions in young Toller. He was in the process of becoming very badly hooked. And it's obvious he needed money to continue the habit. Hence the attack on Mrs Avery. Only his own dabs on the bottle, by the way. These pushers are very careful when they hand the stuff over to a client. Toller was probably given tablets wrapped in a screw of paper.'

'You've heard Miss Sheldon's story of the man known as Chuck, who possesses a knife which could have caused the stab wounds on Arnold Toller's body,' Spratt commented. 'And your witness, Kane, saw a cigarette-smoking woman driving the car. We know Miss Sheldon's Triumph was used in the killing, her description of Chuck tallies with Kane's. So I take it, Mr Joynton, you've established, in your own mind at least, that Arnold Toller was Mrs Avery's attacker and that this Chuck and the woman we know as Mrs Lingford were the principals in Toller's killing?'

'I can't see any flaws in that reasoning,' Joynton returned. 'And what I'm left with is the job of running down the killer and his associates.'

'In whom we're also interested,' Spratt said, 'because of their drug-pushing organisation. So we co-operate. But the entire gang seem to have disappeared, which means we're short of a definite lead.'

'If we could only lay our hands on those two girls. Thompson and Hathorn, sir,' Brenda put in, 'it's possible they could tell us something. It's rather odd they haven't been found yet. They must be lying very low somewhere.'

'Their homes are being watched, of course,' Spratt returned, 'and every policeman in the region has been alerted to keep an eye open for them. They'll be turned up eventually, but meantime — .' One of the telephones on his desk began to ring. He picked it up, said, 'Just a second,' and beckoned to Garrett. 'For you.'

Garrett got up, took the receiver, announced himself. The others waited while he punctuated his caller's conversation with a series of monosyllables.

215

Finally, with a 'Thank you very much, Mr Pearson, you've been most helpful,' he put the receiver down.

'That was the farmer Brenda and I met, sir,' he explained to Spratt. 'He offered to get the present address of the man who owns the field where the caravan was, the said owner, Makin, being away on holiday.'

'That's where the fellow with the rifle — Kit, wasn't it? — was hanging out for some days?'

'Correct, sir. A neighbour is looking after Makin's stock while he is away. Makin had left his address and a phone number where he could be reached in case of emergency. Pearson got on the line to him.

'Makin was approached last Friday by a man who gave his name as Christopher Bradley. Makin's description of him fits the man Miss Sheldon knows as Kit. He told Makin he was proposing to hire a caravan and he needed permission to put it in Makin's field, offering to pay for the privilege, of course. Makin agreed to this. Bradley said a Deniston caravan-hire firm would tow out the caravan to the field the following Monday — that's last Monday, of course. Bradley also enquired if there was any chance for a bit of rough shooting and Makin said he was welcome to keep down any rabbits he saw around. Hence, I suppose, sir, the excuse for the sporting rifle.

'But the point which interested me most was this. Makin mentioned that he'd crossed the field one afternoon and Canfield, the landlord of the Red Lion, had been talking to Bradley at the caravan. Makin got the impression they knew each other quite well. Yet Canfield denied all knowledge to us of a man named Kit.'

'So it seems,' Joynton said, 'that Canfield must be talked to again. And the sooner the better.'

'I agree, of course,' Spratt replied, 'though at the same time, it mightn't pay to be too precipitate. It's the organizers of this gang we're after, and to rattle up one or two of the subordinates might send the principals right underground.'

'There is that point,' Joynton conceded.

'Canfield seems to have been a little suspicious of his two visitors — Garrett and Miss Sheldon — this morning. Further probing would naturally tend to harden those suspicions. Though there is the chance, you know, that he could provide a good lead.'

'If I might make a suggestion, sir.' Brenda looked at Spratt, who nodded.

'Would it be possible to use Dave Morgan's boys here? I know they do go in for weekend camping, and it's not too late in the season for that. If we could arrange for them to camp in the field where the caravan was, they'd keep an eye on Canfield for us. Or would you object to bringing in civilians to help us?'

Joynton seemed about to speak, then thought better of it. Spratt frowned thoughtfully before he replied.

'It's an idea, Brenda. I'll have to consider it.' He pushed his chair away from the desk. 'We've spent enough time talking things over. I know Mr Joynton is eager to get back to his own Division. Norwood, you find out who hired Bradley the caravan and see what you can dig out about him.'

'Yes, sir,' Norwood responded, and was first out of the room. In the general office he settled down to his task. It proved a short one; the second firm he tried, Banks and Leach, was able to tell him they had hired a trailer caravan to a Christopher Bradley for three nights from the previous Monday to the Wednesday. On instructions, they had towed it to a field near Brandsfield and had collected it again that morning. Bradley had given his address as 14 St Stephen's Street, Deniston.

'Could you give me a description of this man?' Norwood asked the girl to whom he had been talking.

'I'm afraid not, sir. I've been getting the information you required from our office records. Mr Leach dealt with the customer. Would you like to speak to him?'

'I'll call in and have a word with him in ten minutes or so.' St Stephen's Street was only a stonesthrow away from Banks and Leach. He went down to his car.

Mr Leach, tall and thin, with a hawklike face and alert eyes, came forward, in an immaculate white coat, to meet him from a large showroom filled with gleaming new cars and caravans. He shook hands with a salesman's hearty grip.

'So our customer was a wrong 'un, eh, Sergeant?' he began. 'Well, we get all sorts, you know. But at any rate, he didn't bilk us. We saw to that, of course. He paid his deposit — which by the way, he hasn't been back to collect yet — and the price of the hire, all in good treasury notes.'

'It's just a case of hoping Bradley can help us with some enquiries we're making, sir. I'm on my way to the address he gave you, but I'd like to be sure he's the man I want to see. Could you describe him to me?'

'Fairly well, I think.' Leach launched himself into a description which tallied, quite accurately, with the one Brenda had given. 'He came here twice, you see. Last Friday, to arrange about hiring the van, and on Monday he rode out to his camping spot with one of our men who towed the van there for him.'

'Did your man bring him back when he picked up the caravan this morning?'

'He didn't. He found a note pinned to the van door which said the hirer had been called away on business, and wouldn't need a lift back.'

'Could I have a look at the caravan he hired, sir?'

'Nothing easier. Just step this way.'

The small cream-coloured caravan, a two-berth job, was standing in a yard at the rear of the premises. Leach unlocked it, moved aside to let Norwood enter. In less than a minute the Regional man was convinced Bradley had taken care to leave no traces behind him. Leach, standing in the doorway, asked, 'Notice anything odd, Sergeant?'

'There doesn't seem to be anything to notice at all, sir. Obviously, as soon as a van comes back, you clean it out and tidy it up ready for the next customer.'

'That's just the point. This van hasn't been touched since our man towed it back. And yet it's in the mint condition it was when it went out last Monday.

'Now, of course, you get all sorts of hirers of caravans. Some take the trouble to leave everything as they found it and others — well, you'd think they'd kept pigs in the van. But no matter how careful clients are, they always leave some signs of occupation behind them, if it's only a cup misplaced on a shelf or a wrinkle in one of the bunk covers. Yet this van looks as if the chap who hired it never used it at all.'

Norwood didn't comment on that. 'Do you know what sort of luggage he took with him?'

'I do, because I saw him into the car. He had a suitcase and some sort of a gun, or to be more accurate, a rifle by the shape of it, in a canvas case.'

Norwood walked back to the show-room with Leach, thanking him for his time and trouble and deftly parrying the questions the car salesman put to him as to his precise interest in Christopher Bradley.

St Stephen's Street was a long uphill street of terrace houses, their front doors opening directly on to the pavement. His knock brought the shuffle of slippered feet to the door. Then it was opened a crack and a large round face, brown-eyed and surmounted by a mass of blonde hair with greying roots, peered out at him.

Norwood proferred his warrant card, which was examined closely through the aperture.

'Police, eh? What's it all about, then?'

'I'm looking for Mr Christopher Bradley, madam. Is he at home?'

'He isn't, because he doesn't live here. What makes you think he did?'

'He gave this as his address when he hired a caravan from Banks and Leach recently, madam.'

'Our Kit hire a caravan? You must be crazy. What would he want to do a thing like that for?' The door was opened wider.

'I've no idea, madam. You said 'our Kit.' Could I have your name?'

'Connor,' she said sulkily. 'Annie Connor.'

Norwood repressed a start. After all, coincidences did happen. He said, casually, 'Have you any relations in the catering business?'

'Me husband has a caff in Lambert Street. You may know it. The Groove Caff. Why?'

'I know The Groove. I just wondered — about your name, I mean. Now, this Mr Bradley I'm wanting to contact, Mrs Connor. You referred to him just now as if he were a relation, too.'

'He's me brother.'

'But he doesn't live here. Perhaps you'd be good enough to give me his present address?'

He saw suspicion cloud her heavy features.

'Just what do you want him for?'

'We think he may be able to help us to trace a certain man we're anxious to lay hands on, Mrs Connor.'

'Oh . . . You said something about him hiring a caravan and giving this address, didn't you? I can't understand that, either. What he'd want one of them things for I can't imagine. Anyway, why didn't he use his own address?'

Norwood fancied he could guess the answer to that one. If Bradley were on some illegal game, he'd have the crook's instinct to confuse his tracks as much as possible. When asked for his address by the hire firm, he'd play cautious and give a false one. The first street name and number which would come into his head, likely enough, would be his sister's. A trivial, senseless trick, but the sort a wrongdoer would play almost without thinking.

'He probably had some good reason,' he said vaguely. 'Anyway, where does he live?'

'Bay Horse Hotel — that's in Royal Square. It's not much of a place, but Kit's not married and it seems to suit him.'

'What's his job, Mrs Connor?'

'Oh . . . Well, he never was what you'd call a settled type, our Kit. He's done all sorts. Lorry driving, baker's roundsman, night watchman — that sort of thing.'

'He's never fancied helping your husband at The Groove?'

'He did try it for a while, but he didn't like it. Mind you, him and my husband have always got on well together, I'll say that for them. Anyway, I've told you where our Kit hangs out now.'

Norwood grinned at her. 'In other words, Mrs Connor, if I want to know more, why don't I ask your brother himself? Fair enough.'

He turned away, went back to his car and drove to Royal Square.

Despite its high-sounding name, the square was not in one of Deniston's most thriving areas. Situated well to the west of the city centre, it was run down, uncared for, on its last legs. It wouldn't be long, Norwood thought, before all these Victorian buildings fell into the grip of demolition, and for his taste, the sooner the better. The Bay Horse Hotel was poked away in one corner of the square, a free house probably being run on a shoe-string by an owner who was hanging on for the compensation he could screw out of the Corporation when he had to move in accordance with its redevelopment plans.

It was just after six, the bar was open but he seemed to be its first customer. He bought half a pint of bitter which he didn't want from a bony, dark-skinned young woman who served him sullenly.

Norwood didn't introduce himself officially. He took the top off what proved to be very inferior beer and asked if Kit Bradley was around.

'He isn't.'

'But he lives here, doesn't he?'

'So what? He went off last weekend, if you must know, and he hasn't been back since.'

'You mean he's left here permanently?'

'I didn't say that. He's keeping his room on.' The woman turned away to pick up the evening paper lying on the bar counter.

'Bad luck for me. I'll have to call in again sometime.' He bade her goodnight without receiving any reply and went out, leaving his glass still half full. And that's it for today, he told himself as he drove homewards.

14

Having dealt effectively with the sports-
man at the gate of the abandoned farm
the previous Wednesday, Elsie Thompson
and Jean Hathorn had cast themselves
into the hedge bottom the moment they
felt they were out of sight and out of
range of a rifle bullet. They lay there,
panting both from their run and from
sheer fright. Elsie was the first to recover.

'Blimey, Jean, that was close. I was
expecting a slug through me pants every
second, wasn't you?'

Jean nodded. 'Think he'll come chasing
after us?'

'Not him. It's Miss Sheldon what they
want, not us.' She raised her head. 'Look,
we'd better get into that wood yonder.
We'll be okay there.'

The wood was thick, heavy with
undergrowth of bracken, brambles,
clumps of thorn and wild roses. They
wriggled under the barbed wire fence

which guarded it and found a grass-grown ride which ran the entire length of the covert.

'Coo!' Elsie exclaimed. 'Look at all these bleeding blackberries! Come on, let's get a bellyful of 'em.'

'Make a change from raw turnips and them sour apples we got in that old orchard,' Jean agreed. 'Though me, I could fancy a nice plate o' fish and chips just now. Hey, what's that you got in your hand?'

'That big bloke's knife, what I used to cut Miss Sheldon free with. Might come in useful y'know.' She slid the knife into the pocket of her dress.

'And what,' Jean enquired an hour later, when they'd eaten their fill of blackberries and explored the wood, 'are we going to do now? I mean, we can't keep on the run for ever, can we?'

'We ain't giving ourselves up yet, if that's what you mean. Not while this lot lasts.' With an air of triumph she produced some treasury notes and fluttered them in front of Jean's eyes.

'Crimes! Where did you get them from?'

'That bloke I laid out in the stable. While you was keeping watch at the door, I rolled him for his wallet. Seven pound ten here. We c'n go places with it.'

'Go where, 'xactly? That's what I want to know.'

'I got a plan all made. If it works out, we'll never see flamin' Westwood again. You trust me, Jean. First off, though, we're going back to yon farm.'

'You must be crazy!'

'I'm not, you know. Time's getting on, and we've got to have somewhere to stay the night. And that there loft was comfortable.'

'But the gang what was there! If they spot us again . . . '

'We'll have to see they don't. Me, I reckon they'll be moving outa that place soon. And, even if Miss Sheldon gets clear of 'em, the cops won't likely be round till tomorrow. Let's go.'

Doubtfully, Jean followed her out of the wood and back by the hedgeside. Halfway along it, Elsie grabbed her arm.

'There's that fellow with the gun, just going through the gate. Only, he's got a sort of case on the gun now. Hey, let's follow him, see where he goes.'

'Not me, Jean said firmly. 'I've seen enough of that devil.'

'Then you stay here, else go back into the wood.' Elsie was off at once, deaf to Jean's protests. With a wary eye lifting towards the farm, which showed no signs of life now, Elsie followed her quarry cautiously along the road. He tramped on without looking back. He reached the main road, turned left. Elsie ran forward to the junction and peered round it. Some two hundred yards away was a road-side pub, quite a smart affair, she thought, from what she could see of it. She watched the man knock at the closed front door. He was admitted almost immediately, as if he had been expected. Elsie walked along until she could see the name of the pub, then turned and hurried back to her friend.

'Thought you was never coming,' Jean grumbled. She was still cowering behind the tree. 'Look, I can't stick much more o' this sorta going-on. Maybe we'd better give ourselves up.'

Elsie ignored this. 'I'll bet odds on that lot have left the farm now, Jean. See, we'll nip across this next field and come on it from the back, like we did when we first found it. Say there's nobody there now — and I'm telling you there won't be — we'll wash ourselves up at that pump and then we'll have a little walk.'

'Walk? Where to?'

'Place called Brandsfield. It's only a mile. I seen a signpost at the end of the road. There'll be some sort of a shop there, even if they don't run to a chippery. We'll buy food and come back here for the night. Tomorrow — well, I got plans about that, like I said.'

'And you haven't told me what they are.'

'Later. Come on!'

They circled the farm with care, but it was soon obvious the birds who had made it their temporary nest had now flown. The cars had gone from the barn, there were no signs of life about the place at all.

They made their way into the house, to find it empty. There was a dried-up scrap of soap in a sink, Jean found part of a torn sheet, not too grimy, thrown down at the back of a cupboard. They washed at the pump, tidied their hair and brushed each other down as well as they could.

'I just got one other thing to do before we set off,' Elsie said. She went out to search round the buildings till she found a broken roof tile. On it she scratched the message which Brenda found the following day.

'I reckon that's damn daft,' Jean said, watching her. 'Look, we don't want to get mixed up any more with what's bin going on here. 'Sides, that Sheldon bitch is a cop. And you're supposed to hate cops as much as I do, Elsie. So why help 'em?'

'Miss Sheldon may be a woman scuffer, but she's a decent sort,' Elsie rejoined. 'And if you had anything inside that loaf of yours, Jean Hathorn, you'd see that giving the fuzz a bit of help this way'll likely do us some good. So shut up. I'm putting this in that room upstairs, where they'll be likely to find it if they come to search this spot. Be down in a second.'

They left the farm, reached the main road and turned in the direction of Brandsfield. Passing the Red Lion was tricky, since it was still broad daylight. They walked on the far side of the road and kept their faces turned away. As far as they could judge nobody saw them.

Brandsfield proved to be a small place, a one-street village, but its three modest shops took care of the girls' immediate needs. They bought bread, butter and a piece of cheese from one, two pork pies from a second. The third provided them with chocolate and bottles of Coca Cola. They didn't linger in Brandsfield, nobody looked at them suspiciously nor asked any awkward questions. They slipped away from the village like the wild creatures they had become accustomed to imitate and passed the Red Lion as safely as before. The farm was still deserted when, in the falling dusk they circled it cautiously. They climbed to the stable loft, burrowed into the hay it contained and ate and drank luxuriously.

'Now,' Elsie said as she brushed crumbs from her dress and lay back comfortably. 'I'll tell you, Jean, about them plans what I mentioned. You ever heard of a woman called Molly Bilton?'

'Never.'

'Well, listen. This Molly Bilton's old man, he was on the crook. And he was a proper pro at it. Me dad worked with him once. Then old Jack Bilton's missus died and Jack smashed hisself up for good in his car. And there was this daughter, Molly, see, as carried on her dad's business. Did one or two smart jobs, too, till she nearly got caught and then she packed it in and went legit. She paid off the fellers as had worked for her and me dad was one.

'That's how I know all this, from hearing me dad on about her to me mum, see? And I remember he said when Molly retired she went to live at a spot called Wellesbourne Green. The name sorta stuck in me mind, like, it's kinda pretty when you say it. She started up one of these riding schools there. It's a place about halfway between Leeds and York.'

Jean yawned. 'Can't see what all this has got to do with us.'

'We're going there tomorrow. We got the dough to take us there now. And we see this Molly Bilton and I tell her Ben Thompson's me old man and she helps us out for the sake of old times.'

'Why the 'ell should she do that?'

'Because me dad said, like father, like daughter. Old Jack Bilton 'ud always help anybody what had worked for him, and me dad reckoned Molly would, too. It's worth a try, Jean.'

'And how do you reckon she could help me and you?'

'Oh, I dunno. Maybe give us a job at this riding school. Anyway, she'll think of something, you bet. Now let's get ourselves some kip.'

They were away from the farm early the next morning. Elsie had enquired about bus times into Deniston from Brandsfield the previous evening, and they joined the queue at the stop in the middle of the village street just before half-past eight. Nobody seemed to take the slightest notice of them.

At the Deniston bus station a departure board told them where to go for the Wellesbourne Green bus, they had only a few minutes to wait. The bus was a single-decker, clearly one doing a country round. There was no conductor, they paid their fares to the driver as they got in and he was too busy with his ticket machine and money bag to do more than nod when Elsie asked him to let them know when they reached Wellesbourne Green.

They reached their destination just after ten o'clock. It was another small village, with a twisting street which was almost deserted at that time of day. Elsie spoke to an old man who was leaning over the gate of a cottage.

'We're looking for a Miss Bilton,' she told him. 'Could you tell us where we can find her?'

'Ah, that'll be her at the riding stables, m'dear. Go past the post office yonder and you'll find a lane running off. Straight down there, you can't miss it.'

Elsie sad, 'Thanks, dad,' and, just beyond where the lane bent out of sight of the village street, they came upon double white gates and a sign which said, 'Wellesbourne Green Riding School. Prop. M. Bilton.' They saw a gravelled drive, flanked by lawns and flower borders, which led to a small, neat bungalow. Set back behind it was a long range of buildings and, over a clipped hedge, was a field dotted with jumps of various heights and types. Elsie grinned.

'Looks as if she's done very well for herself. And all from what her old man made outa crime. And they say it doesn't pay!'

'Look,' Jean said, 'I don't like this much. S'pose, now she's gone legit, she turns us in?'

'We'll have to risk it, won't we?' But now it came to the point of issue, Elsie wasn't feeling too sure herself. Then a man walked round the side of the bungalow carrying a rake. He gave a glance at them before he began to smooth out the hoof-marked gravel of the drive.

Elsie pushed one of the gates open, marched up to the man, with Jean trailing reluctantly behind her. He leaned on his rake to watch them approach.

'Morning,' Elsie said. 'Miss Bilton at home?'

'Just got back from exercise, miss. You'll find her in the stables, I shouldn't wonder.' He gestured towards one end of the bungalow.

Elsie thanked him and they followed a path which led them into a wide cobbled yard, surrounded on three sides by horse boxes, on the fourth by a feed store and tack room. A man stood holding a chestnut horse in the yard while a woman, bare-headed, in a high-necked white sweater and jodpurs was running long slender fingers down the chestnut's near foreleg. She straightened up.

'He's all right, Jim,' she said. 'I gave him plenty to do this morning and that leg's as good as ever now. You can take him away.' As she turned she saw the two girls, smiled, and came towards them.

Molly Bilton, now in her late twenties, was brown-haired, tall, with a figure which couldn't be faulted. Blue-grey eyes and a perfect mouth set off a peaches-and-cream complexion which owed nothing to a beautician. She was lovely indeed, in any man's book, but she was no wax model. Those eyes, alert with intelligence, could harden pitilessly on occasion, the firm chin beneath that beautiful mouth could set to granite hardness. Molly was nobody's fool. That was why, when commonsense insisted, she had slid out from the manner of life her adored father had followed, to take up a business she had always secretly longed to do, for Molly was an ardent horse-lover.

'Good morning,' she greeted her two visitors. 'Looking for me? I'm Molly Bilton.' And her eyes, summing up the pair, were a shade puzzled. These girls hardly looked the type who had come to fix up riding lessons.

Elsie called upon all her courage. 'My name's Thompson, miss. Elsie Thompson. My dad used to work for your dad. You know, that job in Manchester, and that 'un in Newcastle. Thought a lot of me old man, your dad did.'

Molly regarded her gravely. 'I remember Ben Thompson very well, of course. He once saved my life — did you know that?' At Elsie's shake of the head she went on, 'No, you wouldn't. Ben never was a boaster. How is he these days?'

'He's fine, miss. Doing five at Leeds Prison. He'll be out round about Christmas next year if he be'aves hisself.'

'And what can I do for his daughter Elsie and her friend?'

'Ah, well, you see, me and Jean — Jean Hathorn's her name — we got into a bit of bother, like, and ended up at yon approved school at Westwood. Only, we didn't like it much, so we sorta left. We bin away nearly a week.'

Molly smiled briefly. 'You look like it. So you've discovered where I live and I suppose you've come here hoping for a handout?'

Elsie looked as indignant as she knew how. 'Oh, no, miss. Nothing like that. We got money, only, we have to lie low for a few more days till the heat's off and we thought maybe you . . . '

'You're asking me to harbour a couple of girls on the run?'

Elsie grinned widely at her now. 'That was the idea, miss.'

Molly said, 'You know, you do remind me of your father. We'll go into the house and — oh, drop calling me 'miss' all the time, would you, Elsie? 'Molly' will do, and that goes for your friend too, if she ever does speak at all.'

'She's a bit shy, miss — Molly, I mean. She isn't as dumb as she looks, really.'

They followed Molly into an apartment which was half sitting room, half office. There was a businesslike desk in one corner with a filing cabinet behind it. There was also a comfortable three piece suite and a low table with a stack of magazines on it beside a glowing fire. All round the room the walls held drawings, paintings and photographs of horses.

Molly told them to sit down, she cleared the small table and set it between them. 'I'm going to brew some coffee,' she said. 'Shan't be long. Just make yourselves at home.'

Elsie winked triumphantly at Jean as the door closed.

'There, what did I tell yer? Cushy pad she's got eh? We'll be okay here.'

'She's right nice,' Jean conceded. 'But

she's not promised us anything, has she?'

'Give her a chance,' Elsie returned, and the conversation died until their hostess reappeared, laden with a coffee tray and a plate of chocolate biscuits.

'Now,' she said when they were both supplied and she had filled her own cup, 'let's have the story, from the time you last saw Westwood.'

It was Elsie who did the talking, of course. She made quite a good job of it, and Molly seemed particularly interested when she heard of the girls' adventures at the farm.

'Just describe that woman you saw there, as clearly as you can,' she said when Elsie had done. 'And the man who kept watch on the policewoman you mentioned.'

Elsie looked doubtful but Jean cut in at once. It was clear when she had finished speaking that though her tongue was somewhat backward in use, there was nothing wrong with her sense of observation.

'That's fine,' Molly said. 'I think I know the woman, and a nasty piece of work she is. I'm not definitely sure about the man you saw with her, but I'll bet your big chap, the man who was left on guard, is an old acquaintance of mine. If I'm right, he's an ex-wrestler, used to perform under the name of the Brummagem Buster. Not a bad fellow, really, but dim as they come. His real name is Dan Siggins.'

'Here, half a minute!' Elsie exclaimed. 'Look at this.' She hauled Buster's knife from her pocket. 'This belonged to the big guy, I used it to cut Miss Sheldon free and then I sorta absentmindedly hung on to it. There's a bit of silver stuff let into the handle. Says 'D.S.' on it.'

Molly took the knife, looked at it, handed it back.

'Now, see here,' she said. 'Sooner or later, you two will be caught and sent back to Westwood. You realise that, don't you?'

'Oh, but Molly — '

'It's no use, Elsie. It's bound to happen, and you know it. Now, I'm not going to turn you in myself, you can lie low here for a few days, say till over the weekend. You've obviously been living rough lately and a rest and some decent food will do you both good. After that, you move on. Understand?'

The pair nodded in unison. Even Elsie realised there was no point in trying to argue.

'I have an extra bedroom you can use and you'll have your meals in the house with me. If you like, you can help around the place to fill in time. But only till Monday morning, remember. Now I'll show you the bathroom, you both look as if you could use it!'

15

When the girls had disappeared, Molly went to her desk and sat there, leaning back and staring thoughtfully at the ceiling. Elsie and Jean, by their presence here and, more important, by the story they had told, had forced her back into a past which she had thought she had put behind her for keeps, a past which would never intrude on her again.

She had adored her dead father, Jack Bilton. He had worked outside the law because that was the path he had deliberately chosen. Because it had been an absorbing path for him, it had been absorbing for Molly as a child, as an adolescent, as a grown woman. Jack had organised his various jobs with all the efficiency his keen brain had brought to them; once or twice he had been unlucky, and had paid for it. But he had never allowed violence to enter his schemes, and he had been as loyal to the men and women who worked for him as they had been loyal to him. It had seemed natural to Molly to carry on, in her early twenties, where her father had left off.

Then, quite suddenly, she had had a change of heart. There had been an occasion when she had sailed far too close to the wind for comfort. This was not the life, she realised, to which she wanted to devote herself completely, as her father had done. She had disbanded the organisation he had set up, with handsome compensations to the people who had been part of that organisation. And then, always a lover of horses, she had set up the riding school here, and had made it pay. Her natural energy and business acumen had seen to that.

But now the past had reached out, laid a hand on her shoulder. Like the two girls who had descended upon her, she had no clear idea of the objects of the gang which had used the derelict farm as a temporary headquarters, but she had very strong suspicions of the sort of traffic the woman Jean had described was engaged in. It was something any decent person would be eager to stop, even at personal risk.

She moved suddenly in decision, took a bunch of keys from her breeches pocket and unlocked a drawer in her desk. From it she took a small notebook, rifled through the pages until she found a name, and then she pulled the desk telephone towards her and began to dial.

★ ★ ★

Garrett looked up from his work as Brenda Sheldon came into the main office at Kingsmead House.

'I thought you were still on leave. Can't you stay away from this spot, love? I only wish I had the chance myself.'

'I just dropped in to say I've fixed that business with Dave Morgan. He's going to organise a camping weekend for a group of his lads in the field next to the Red Lion.'

'So you sold your idea to the bosses?'

Brenda nodded. 'Mr Hallam agreed, after Mr Spratt and I talked to him. It's a bit unorthodox, using civilians like that, but as Mr Hallam said, we're not tied to normal routine here. Has anything else happened?'

'Not a thing. Barry's still out on that assignment, chasing up Bradley by way of the caravan hire firm, we've heard nothing further from Joynton.'

'Then I'll leave you to it, Dick. I'm on my way to the hospital to see Aunt Gertrude — Mrs Avery, that is.'

'She's going on all right?'

'Probably will be sent home tomorrow. Be seeing you.'

Garrett returned to his mass of paper work. As he began to fill in a form his desk telephone rang.

'Call for you, Sergeant,' the switch-board operator said. 'A Miss Molly Bilton. Okay to put her through?'

'Sure.' Garrett was suddenly conscious that his pulse-rate had jerked up. Molly Bilton, eh? That was one right out of the blue.

He announced himself, and heard the rich tones he remembered so well.

'I don't know if you'll recollect my name, Sergeant. We met at Whitsea some four years ago.'

Garrett chuckled. 'How could I ever forget it? You got out of that business rather well, didn't you? Conditional discharge, I believe. How's business going these days?

'Very well, I'm glad to say. But not the sort of business you're thinking about. I — er — retired from that after Whitsea.'

'I'm glad to hear it. And what are you doing now?'

'Running a livery stables and riding school at Wellesbourne Green. But this isn't a social call, Sergeant. I understand you're interested in an old farmhouse near Brandsfield?'

'We are.' Garrett reverted at once to the policeman, alert, wary.

'I have some information which might be of use to you, but first I want to know what the suspected offence is.'

'I'm afraid I can't tell you that, Miss Bilton.'

'You can at least confirm my own suspicions. It it connected in any way with pushing drugs?'

'It's just possible.' That was safely non-committal, anyway.

'Which is good enough for me. So you get your information.

'Fire away, then, Miss Bilton.'

'I can't, not at the moment. I've gathered some, but not enough to be of any value to you. The rest of it I hope to have by tomorrow. And I'd rather not telephone it. I suggest we meet somewhere, preferably tomorrow evening.'

'In Deniston? Or at your place?'

'I'll come to town.'

'Good. What about dinner at The Yorkist, in Greville Street? I'm told they do you pretty well there.'

'That would be delightful. Shall we say eight o'clock?'

Garrett agreed, and with a 'Till then,' Molly cut them off. He sat motionless in his chair for some minutes, wondering what he had let himself in for. It was advisable for a young police officer, keen on promotion, to steer entirely clear from such girls as Molly Bilton, even if . . . He stretched out a hand suddenly for the telephone directory, to book a table for two at The Yorkist.

He arrived there at a quarter to eight

the following evening, with a long frustrating day behind him. But now, he thought, he could forget all the irritations for a while. There was nothing more relaxing than the company of a beautiful young woman in an atmosphere of good food and drink. Whether his expense sheet would stand for it or not, Garrett meant to enjoy himself.

But when Molly turned up, dead on time, she seemed in rather a sombre mood. Garrett thought she looked smashing, the dress she was wearing was exactly right, she had nothing to learn about the art of make-up and he was proud indeed to walk into the diningroom at her side. Yet something was troubling her, that was obvious. She made an effort to respond to his light, teasing conversation, she tried to conceal her lack of appetite.

They took their coffee in the lounge. Garrett waited until his companion had sipped at hers and then he leaned forward.

'This is where we get down to business, Molly.' They had agreed on first-name terms during the early part of their dinner. Molly nodded.

'I said I had some information for you, Dick. You'll want all of it, chapter and verse, and that's going to make things difficult. I'm right out of the game now, and I'm staying that way. But, you know, there are such things as loyalties.'

'What you're saying is that you want to keep old friends of yours out of trouble. I'm sorry, Molly, but if any of them are in this particular racket, I'll do my personal best to see they suffer. And that goes for all the people who work for me.'

Molly smiled briefly. 'That's hardly the attitude a cop usually takes when he wants information out of a grasser, is it? But, look. It is a drug-pushing job, isn't it?'

Garrett nodded. 'And to me that's the filthiest form of crime. In my book it rates lowest.'

'In mine, too. That's why I want to help, only, Dick, it's got to be in my own way. What do you know about these people?'

'We know a fair bit about some of the

underlings, but it's the big ones we want — and how!'

Molly asked quietly, 'Does the name Hester Banning mean anything to you?'

Garrett shook his head. 'Not a thing. Should it?'

'Maybe. What about a man — Chuck Stevens?'

'Ah!' Garret's eyes lit up. 'That's better. A character called Chuck — don't know his second name — has come to our notice. I can describe him, at second hand. About medium size, wiry, tough-looking. Protruding teeth. Carries a shiv.'

'That's Stevens,' Molly agreed. 'He always was a knife man. Any other names you know?'

Garrett felt he was committed now. 'A woman, Mrs Lingford. A big hulking chap called Buster, a rat-like fellow known as Smedley, and a sporting sort of type, Christopher Bradley.'

He was watching Molly carefully as he spoke, but she showed no reaction to any of the four names he gave. All she said was, 'I mentioned Hester Banning just now. She's tall, slender, brown hair, pale eyes, pointed chin. And she's a chain-smoker.'

'That's an exact description of a woman we're looking for, though she was wearing a black wig when last seen. But we know her as Mrs Lingford.'

'So that's what she's calling herself these days? And Chuck Stevens was working with her?'

'He was. Of course, we've checked with Records, but we couldn't get anything on a Mrs Lingford.'

'You try the name I've given you, Dick. You'll find enough there to convince you she's the dirtiest piece of work you've ever come across.'

She rose in one swift movement. 'Thanks for the dinner, and the company, Dick. You must come out and see my little place sometime.'

Garrett was also on his feet. 'But you're not going yet, surely? what about all this information you promised me?'

'I've told you all I can tonight. Give me until tomorrow and I hope I'll have some really hard news for you then. I can get you at your H.Q.?'

'Yes, But, see, Molly — '

'It's no use, Dick This has got to be played my way. You can see me to my car if you like. But don't bother to tail me. I'm going straight home to Wellesbourne Green.'

16

Molly indeed drove directly home, but she left her car standing on the drive in front of the house instead of putting it away. There was a light on in the lounge and when she entered the room it was to find Elsie and Jean stretched out on their stomachs in front of the fire, playing pontoon for matches. Elsie looked up at her.

'Gee, Molly, you do look lovely! See, when I get my hands on a bit of lolly, I'm buying a dress just like that. It's fab!'

'Flattery,' Molly said, 'will get you nowhere, young lady, except where you ought to be — in bed. It's long past ten o'clock, and you still need plenty of sleep.'

Jean was counting matches into piles of ten. She glanced up to say, 'You been out with a boy friend, haven't you? You got that look in yer eye. Nice, was he?'

'He was nice, he wasn't a boy friend.

Now, off to bed, both of you.'

They scrambled up obediently, said goodnight to Molly and disappeared, Their hostess opened the glass doors of a bookcase, found a large-scale map and spread it out on her desk. She searched for and found a name — Lyndonthorpe. Then she set herself to work out a route which would take her there — just over thirty miles from Wellesbourne Green. She pencilled the various roads lightly in on the map, memorising them as the pencil point traced them out.

At a quarter to eleven she went into her bedroom. Here she changed into slacks, a high-necked sweater and stout shoes. She eased open the door of the girls' room and listened. They both seemed soundly asleep. She shrugged herself into her suede leather car coat, turned off the lights and went out to her car. The engine, still warm, fired quietly. Molly drove to the road, turned left. The sky was overcast but visibility was good. With luck, she should reach Lyndonthorpe by midnight.

A church clock was striking twelve

when she drove into a small village. Lyndonthorpe's one main street was unlighted and there were no signs of life in the cottages and farmhouses which bordered it. Molly's headlights showed her a stretch of tree-dotted grass to her left. She pulled her car on to the grass, ran it under the shelter of a tree and cut the engine. She stepped out of the car and locked it, dropping the keys into a pocket of her coat. She stood still, letting her vision adjust itself to her surroundings.

Facing her across the stretch of grass was a high wall. She moved quietly along a footpath under this wall, to the far end of the village, where a church tower stood up against the night sky. Passing the church, she came to a wide iron gate at the end of a drive shrouded with thick conifers. This was Lyndonthorpe Rectory, but no parson lived there now. The sprawling Tudor-built house was too big for a country cleric to run in these servantless days.

The gate was padlocked. Molly climbed over it and landed lightly on the drive which, once gravelled, was now a mere stretch of beaten-down earth. She took a small torch from her pocket and went on through a tunnel of darkness, with the torch beam directed a few feet in front of her. Some ten yards from the gate her light picked up what she had expected, a trip wire at ankle level. She stepped carefully over it. There weren't likely to be any more traps on this drive, but she took no chances. She came out from under the trees without finding another wire. She stood still again, her eyes roving over the mass of the building in front of her. Not a gleam showed from any of its windows.

Yet, if the information she had received that day were correct, she was looking at the place where the rats had gone to earth. The rats Dick Garrett and his colleagues were seeking and which she herself would be glad to exterminate — all except one. She had learnt that Hester Banning and her crowd had taken over the empty rectory at Lyndonthorpe, their front being that they wished to set up a private school there. And her old friend Dan Siggins, universally nick-named Buster, was one of that crowd.

Molly had known Buster nearly all her life. He had worked for her father in the intervals of a professional wrestling career which had never amounted to very much. Buster had brawn in plenty, but he was woefully light on brains. Molly's guess was that he'd been conned into this mob as the muscleman they needed. Buster wasn't averse from relieving honest citizens of their money or goods, but he had no record of violence. As for drug trafficking, that wasn't Buster at all. The likelihood was he'd never tumbled to what was really going on, smart operators like Hester Banning and Chuck Stevens could make that big bonehead fall for any yarn. Tell Buster he was needed to rob a bank so that the proceeds could be given to charity and he'd believe it.

Somehow or other, Molly had to get him away from this place, tell him the truth about the racket he'd got into. Then, with a clear conscience as far as she was concerned, she could give Dick Garrett the name of the hideout, and the law would take care of the rest. But she must get in touch with Buster tonight.

The trip wire suggested they wouldn't have any guards out, but she remained where she was, motionless, for a good ten minutes. Still no sign of life nor movement, neither inside nor outside the old rectory. And you had to take risks in a job like this . . .

She walked along the edge of a neglected lawn which fronted the house. Beyond it, a path led through a shrubbery. Molly tried the path, it took her, as she had hoped, round the back of the house. Here there was a paved court surrounded by low buildings, with the churchyard beyond them. Not a light to be seen on this side, either.

She found her way through the courtyard on to a back drive. She went along it, using her torch again. A second trip wire was stretched near the end of the drive where, through a broken wooden gate, it led to the road. She pushed through the gate and walked back to the front drive again.

Before she had met Garrett that

evening, Molly had talked, in a Deniston lodging house, to a small weasel-faced man known as Flick Fawcett. It was he who told her where Buster could be found and Molly had paid him generously for the information. But how to get Buster, probably asleep in that old rectory, awake and out in the open so that she could rush him to her car and away?

And then she saw the answer. There was a way to get that dark house alert, buzzing like an overturned hive of bees.

She climbed the gate again, switched her torch on and walked forward under the trees until she found the trip wire. She bent to examine it. It was set taut enough not to be activated by any small prowling animals of the night; even a cat, touching it, would not set its alarm off. Molly straightened, drew back one foot and swung it at the wire. It collapsed with a metallic ping. She ran hard along the rest of the drive and across the top of the lawn fronting the house. Already there were lights in two of the upper windows. She reached the shrubbery at the end of the house and ducked behind a sprawling laurel just as the front door was flung open and two people appeared on the step, with the hall lights showing them clearly to her.

A man and a woman. Molly recognized Hester Banning. She had put on a long coat and was rapidly tying a head scarf over her hair. The man was also overcoated, his hair stood up, ruffled and spiky. Molly heard the woman's voice.

'Go down towards the gate, Chuck. I'll search the front here.' Two torches flashed out before them and Chuck leapt off the steps. As she was also about to descend, Hester Banning swung round as a third figure came out of the hall.

'What are you doing here, Smedley, you fool?' she demanded. 'Can't you remember orders? Get to the back of the house and cover it, quick!' Then she ran down the steps on to the lawn.

Molly slipped quietly along the shrubbery path. It was clear enough that the plan was to split forces, back and front, if an alarm sounded. Smedley, probably confused by sleep, had taken the wrong route. Molly guessed he would now be joining Buster, the fourth member of the party, on the back drive. And here, if she were lucky, she could separate them, get Buster on his own.

As she rounded the house and came to the rear courtyard, she heard the squeal of a rusty lock. The back door opened, and, as she crouched in the shadow of the outbuildings she saw Smedley emerge, alone. He flashed his torch once round the courtyard, then made his way towards the back drive.

Buster, ever a heavy sleeper, had either not been roused at all, or he was taking his time to join the hunt. He couldn't have come out of the house before Smedley, and Molly didn't think it likely he'd joined the other party. She waited with frantic impatience for Buster to show himself. This was the opportunity she'd hoped for. But seconds, then minutes, passed and still there was no sign of the big man.

So he hadn't heard the alarm, hadn't been wakened. Therefore he was still in the house. Molly made a rapid decision. She ran lightly across the courtyard and through the door which Smedley had left open behind him.

A short flight of stone steps led her into a kitchen, embers in a fireplace were still glowing feebly. Her torch showed her another door, and, opening it, she found herself in a stone-flagged passage, reeking of damp and disuse. At the end of it were stairs, uncarpeted, the treads showing splotches of dried mud. She climbed the stairs, not concerned now with making a noise. There was an unshaded bulb alight on the landing she reached. She switched off her torch, put it in her pocket.

Two doors gave on to the landing. One was open, the room beyond it was lit. She saw a tumbled bed, a man's jacket lying on the floor. The other door was closed. There was a key in its lock, but the handle turned under her fingers when she tried it.

This room was unlit, but the bulb on the landing showed her a bed on which a large form lay, face downwards. This must be Buster, still peacefully asleep. She'd have to wake him, get him up and out. There could be no harm in putting the light on in here. She reached out and pressed the switch.

It was Buster all right. Dressed in shirt and trousers, he lay sprawled on the bed, one arm hanging loosely over its side. Molly took a step forward, then pulled up with a choking gasp. She saw the blood which had soaked, in a large patch, into his white shirt. Then she saw the knife-stab beneath his left shoulder. She knelt to take the suspended hand, her fingers searching for a pulse she knew would not be there. Buster was dead — murdered.

The bedroom door slammed shut behind her. Before she could scramble to her feet the key turned in the lock.

Molly sprang across the room to window, opened it wide. She looked down at the courtyard, a tall storey below. She glanced from left to right, seeking a fall pipe down which she might climb. There wasn't one. Turning her back to the window, she leaned out, looking upwards. Only a bare wall towered above her, reaching to the steep roof above. No help there. The only possible way of escape from this room was to hang by her fingers from the sill and then drop to the courtyard below. And then what? A broken leg, a cracked pelvis? The odds were against her landing unharmed.

Running footsteps sounded on the stairs outside the room. She had almost decided to chance it, had one knee on the window-sill, when the lock clicked back and the door was jerked open. A harsh voice said, 'I wouldn't try it if I were you, lady!'

Molly regained her balance and turned. Chuck Stevens was standing just inside the room, his lips pulled away from his rabbit-teeth in a grin. The light flashed on the knife he held, casually but competently, in his right hand. Then Smedley pushed in beside him, panting.

'Saw her nipping into the 'ouse, I did, Chuck, when I come back after checking there was nobody about on that back drive. Followed her, quiet, like, up here.'

'Go and fetch the boss,' Chuck grated, and as Smedley clattered away, he took another step forward, his grin widening.

'Well, if it isn't Molly Bilton, old Jack's

little girl! Whoever would have thought that, now?'

Molly spoke from behind clenched teeth. 'I always heard you were the murdering type, Stevens. So you killed my old friend Buster? Why, I can't think, but I'll see you put away for life, if it's the last thing I do!'

Chuck waved his unoccupied hand airily. 'Big words! Big words! Maybe you've done the last thing you'll ever do — coming here. We'll have to see about that, won't we?'

He was between her and the door, he wasn't taking his eyes off her for a second. If she tried to grab her torch from her pocket and fling it in his face . . . No, that wouldn't work. Molly's shoulders sagged as she tried to relax.

Then the stairs creaked again as they carried footsteps and Hester Banning came into the room, with Smedley following her. The woman wasted no time.

'Take her into Smedley's room, Chuck, lock her in there. She'll be safe enough till we decide what to do. Smedley will see she doesn't try to make a break downstairs. Get moving!'

Chuck jerked his head at Molly as the rat-like Smedley moved in behind her. She couldn't tackle the three of them. Best to give in for the moment. She was escorted, closely, into the next room, thrust forcibly across its floor. The door banged, a key turned.

Molly recovered her balance, looked around her. The window of the room was curtained with some flimsy, tattered material, but when she pulled this back she found the window was barred. This had once been a children's nursery. It looked out on the back court and the churchyard wall. She was in a trap from which there was no exit. And Buster had been murdered; the recollection hit her with a renewed sense of shock. She sat down on the bed, striving to put her thoughts in order.

She was up against the most unscrupulous, most coldly-violent creature she had ever encountered — Hester Banning. She would hesitate at nothing, not even killing, if this suited her ends . . .

Molly had no idea how long she had been sitting there, thinking desperately, when the door was unlocked and Chuck and Mrs Banning came in. Molly saw Smedley hovering about outside but the door was immediately shut in his face. Chuck set his back to the wall, his knife in his hand. Mrs Banning came forward and looked down at her prisoner. She took a deep drag on the cigarette she held.

'I've heard,' she began, 'that you possess a certain amount of intelligence, Miss Bilton. Therefore you realize, no doubt, just what you've let yourself in for by coming here.' She crossed to the chest of drawers, stubbed out her cigarette in a tin lid which lay there, took out a case and at once lit another smoke.

'Let me give you some facts,' she went on. 'We found your parked car. It had to be yours, because none of the villagers leave cars on that piece of grass all night. My man Smedley is an expert in the art of opening locked cars and in driving them away without needing their keys. On the panel shelf he found an envelope addressed to you, proof that our guess re that vehicle was right. Your car is now in the garage here, safe from prying eyes. We have made an exhaustive search of the grounds and house and we're certain you came here alone.

'You can be here for one purpose only. You discovered your old friend Dan Siggins — Buster — was working for me. You wanted to get him away from my employ in case the police swooped down on us. They won't, you know, but that's beside the point. You managed to get into this house, and you found Buster had had an unfortunate accident.'

'I found Buster had been murdered,' Molly corrected her sharply.

Mrs Banning waved her cigarette. 'Buster had a violent temper at times, as you may know, Miss Bilton. Over a card game he fell out with Chuck Stevens here.' She half turned. 'Give her the facts, Chuck.'

'Came at me like a raging lion, he did,' the man avowed. 'Swore he'd choke the life outa me. Well, you don't argue with a pro ex-wrestler when he's in that mood, lady. I had to draw me knife to defend

272

meself. What he got, he asked for.'

'Apart from the fact that Buster was never hot-tempered nor violent, you don't defend yourself against an attacker by stabbing him in the back,' Molly returned. 'That's the silliest story I've heard for many a long day.'

Chuck shrugged his shoulders and Mrs Banning spoke again.

'Now, having discovered Buster was in my employ, how did you find this place? The answer is simple. You got the information from Flick Fawcett. You met him by appointment in Deniston at half-past seven this evening — or, rather, last evening, as it's already Saturday morning now. Flick told you about this place, you paid him good money for his information. He told you Buster was here, he gathered from you that you wanted to get Buster away. You said you would get in touch with him — Buster — in the morning — today, that is.' She gave a short, harsh laugh.

'You needn't look so surprised, my dear young friend. Flick is also working for me. He told you what you wanted to know because he felt, in the long run, that it was the best move. We have no telephone laid on here, but there's a phone box in the village, and I have an arrangement with Flick to dial its number at eight o'clock precisely every evening. Chuck always stands by for the call — I like to know any Deniston news Flick has picked up.

'So we expected you, but not until this morning. However, I had the trip wires out as an insurance. Which explains just about everything, I think.'

'Except what we're going to do with her,' Chuck put in.

'Yes.' The word came out slowly. 'We could — er — dispose of you, Miss Bilton. There's a vault in the churchyard here which Smedley who, as I've told you, has a talent for these things, finds he can open. We shall lay your friend Buster to rest there at first light today. But I haven't decided yet whether you shall join him immediately. It doesn't suit my plans to leave here just yet — at least, not for a few days. And, possibly, you could be more useful to me alive than dead. As a hostage, perhaps? We shall have to see.'

She yawned delicately and put her cigarette down.

'We could all do with some more sleep. Smedley will be posted outside this door, Miss Bilton, so I advise you not to try anything. A call from him and Chuck will be on the scene at once. Take my advice, make yourself as comfortable as you can, and we'll see what the morning brings forth.'

Chuck opened the door, watching Molly carefully. He followed the woman out and the key turned in the lock. Molly took off her coat, spread it on the bed and lay down on it, trying not to think of a future which was so exceedingly dark and threatening . . .

17

Reluctantly, Elsie Thompson woke to a muffled banging which became more insistent as she lay and listened to it, half stupefied with sleep. She struggled up at last, blinking at the bedside clock. It showed a few minutes past eight. By her side, Jean was still deeply asleep.

'Somebody at the back door,' Elsie muttered to herself, 'and Molly isn't around or she'd have answered it by now.' She shook Jean into consciousness, lunged out of bed and seized the dressing gown Molly had provided to be shared between them. Belting this round her she went, in bare feet and with extremely tousled hair, to the back door.

Jim Makin, Molly's head stableman, stood there. He was a lean middle-aged man whose acquaintance the girls had already made.

'Morning miss,' he said. 'What's happened to Miss Bilton today? She's usually out by seven o'clock and I want to see her about something particular.'

'So she's overslept, Jim. I'll go and wake her up.'

She went to Molly's bedroom door and knocked loudly. There was no response from within. She twisted the handle, opened the door.

No Molly. Bed hadn't been slept in — but, of course, she could have got up early and made her bed . . . But her working clothes were there, neatly folded on a chair. Elsie crossed the room and opened the doors of a big wardrobe.

The previous evening, when Molly had gone out and left the two girls alone, Elsie had had a comprehensive look in every part of the bungalow, including Molly's bedroom. Her object had been sheer curiosity; she had no thoughts of taking, nor interfering with, anything she might find. Though her morals were lax in some respects, she would never steal from a friend.

She had inspected Molly's wardrobe during her tour of the bungalow. She had fingered and admired all the clothes

Molly possessed. She remembered them perfectly. Now she saw the dress Molly had worn the evening before was on a hanger in the wardrobe, but a pair of navy blue tailored slacks which she herself had rather fancied, was missing. She closed the wardrobe, went to a dressing chest and pulled out its top drawer. Last night, a black high-necked sweater had been lying there. It had now gone.

She returned to the back door.

'Miss Bilton doesn't seem to be around the house, Jim. Maybe she's gone out somewhere — here, is her car in the garage?'

'Wasn't there when I came past just now.'

'Well, that explains it, then.'

'But 'tisn't like her to go off early in her car. And it must have been early, because I live just across the road, you know, and I've been up since five. I'd have heard the car going out. She hasn't left a note around anywhere, has she?'

'Might have done. I haven't been in the sitting room where her desk is. Let's go look.'

Jim followed her into the house. 'No note here,' Elsie said. 'Just this map laid out on her desk. So what?'

Jim shrugged. 'Have to wait till she gets back from wherever she's gone, I suppose. I'm off across home now to have some breakfast. See you later.'

He went out. Elsie returned to the desk and bent over the map there. She saw the pencilled line Molly had drawn on it.

Elsie wasn't lacking in intelligence. She was interested in people, shrewd enough to spot reactions. When she had told Molly of their adventures at the derelict farmhouse, had mentioned Buster and shown Molly his knife, she had the impression Molly was worried because Buster was mixed up with that gang. Also, passing the sitting room door the previous day, Elsie had overheard some of Molly's telephone conversation. She'd not been able to make much of it, but she had gathered that Molly was very concerned about Buster, and anxious to get in touch with him.

Elsie slid off the desk where she had been sitting and went into the kitchen, to a mouthwatering smell of coffee, eggs and bacon. With good reason, Jean fancied herself as a cook.

'Just on ready,' she said. 'Get them cornflakes down you, before this lot in me fry pan spoils.'

They sat down at the kitchen table and reached the stage of toast and marmalade before Jean spoke again.

'So what're we going to do with ourselves today, then?'

Elsie swallowed the last of her toast, licked marmalade from her fingers and looked hard and levelly at her friend.

'I'm worried about Molly, Jean. I reckon she could be in dead trouble. From that gang we tangled with. You just listen.'

She told Jean of her suspicions and of the evidence she had to support them. Jean goggled at her.

'So what are we supposed to do about it?'

'I think we ought to go to this Lyndonthorpe spot and try to find her.'

'How far away is it?' Elsie told her and Jean laughed shortly. 'Only about thirty miles? So I s'pose we walk it?'

Elsie jumped up. 'I'm going to have a word with Jim.'

The stableman was already back at work. 'Any signs of Miss Bilton, yet? No? And she hasn't rung up?' Worry creased his leathery face. 'I don't understand this at all.'

'I've got some ideas about it, Jim. Get a load of this.' She told her story as briefly as she could while Jim, leaning against a corn bin, stared his eyes out. When she had finished, he straightened up decisively.

'If you're right, and you sound sure enough, this is a job for the police. Better get on to them straightaway.'

'What? And land Molly into bad trouble if we're wrong after all? I've told you me and Jean scarpered from Westwood, and she knows it, and she's let us stay here because of me dad. But she didn't oughter have, you know. It's against the law.'

'Then there's nothing we can do but hope she'll just turn up all right, sometime?'

'We could go to Lyndonthorpe and have a look round, see if we could find her. You got a car, Jim. You told me so yesterday. So what about it?'

Jim considered for some moments. 'Sounds crazy to me, and yet, I don't know . . . Lyndonthorpe. Say a couple of hours, there and back. I've got plenty to do here, but I suppose it could wait. Saturday's a busy day for us, school-kids coming for riding lessons and that, but my wife's as good with horses as I am and if she'd come across here for a bit . . . She's done it before to help out . . . Look, I'll see if I can fix it up with her. I still think it's a mad idea of yours, but I'd never forgive myself if . . . '

He went off muttering. Elsie returned to the house, to tell Jean to get ready for a trip out. Then she went into the sitting room, picked up the telephone directory and began to turn its pages slowly.

When she had listened to Molly's phone conversation, two days previously, her hostess had rung up a place called Kings-something House and had asked to speak to Detective-Sergeant Garrett. Elsie had remembered his name. Molly had arranged to meet him last night, Elsie knew that was where she had gone, all dressed up, though she herself hadn't mentioned it to Jean. Now, Elsie thought, maybe it would make sense if she could have a word with this Garrett bloke, even if he was a copper.

Her fingers began to move swiftly through the directory pages. She found the section headed 'Police' with the subsection of 'North Central Regional — Kingsmead House.' That was the place. She pulled the telephone towards her and rang the number. Putting on what she hoped was a 'posh' voice when she was connected, she asked for Detective-Sergeant Garrett and was put through to him.

'My name,' she said, 'is Miss Tompkins, Miss Elizabeth Tompkins. I am a friend of Miss Molly Bilton, of Wellesbourne Green. I understand you're the guy — I mean, the fellow — she was out with last night.'

'So, madam?'

'She come — came — home last night,

then went off again. We haven't seen her since. I reckon she's in danger, at a place called Lyndonthorpe, from that gang what was using that old farmhouse — you know.' Nervousness was making Elsie gabble now. 'So I thought I'd get on the blower to you and you'll haveta to do something about it, won't you — and fast.'

She banged the receiver down, panting. She wouldn't tell Jean, nor the stableman, that she'd rung the law as a safety measure; her friend wouldn't like it, and Jim might refuse to drive to Lyndon-thorpe if he knew the police had been alerted. Elsie felt somebody should get there at once, and you couldn't always trust the dicks to take quick action.

Through the window she saw Jim standing by his car in the road in front of his cottage. So he'd made up his mind to go, then. She folded the map on the desk, picked it up, collected Jean, who was still inclined to twitter dubiously, and ran down the drive. The stableman gave them a wry grin.

'I've fixed it up with my wife,' he said,

'so get in. I see you've brought the map. We'll need it, I'm not sure of the route after the first ten miles.'

Elsie got into the back seat, spread the map over her bony knees. Jean sat in front. The car was an aged Austin 35 but it still had vim and vigour under its bonnet. Jim settled down to prove it.

'Hang on,' he warned Jean as he took a sharp left-hand curve on a steep gradient. Jean grabbed at a small plastic bag which the bend had canted out of the dashboard shelf. She caught it near floor level and held it up to peer at it.

'What you carry a bag o' marbles round with you for, Jim?'

He laughed. 'They belong to my lad. He uses them as ammunition. There's his catapult on the shelf there, too. Broke a window yesterday, he did, shooting, so I took it off him and he'll not get it back for a while. Locked it in the car, with his ammo, so he couldn't get at it.'

Elsie spoke severely as Jean returned the bag to the shelf.

'Lads will be lads, you know, Jim. And catty-shooting comes natural to 'em.

Didn't you have a catty when you were a kid?'

'I did that, miss. I could knock a sparrow off at twenty paces. I've hit running rats, as well.' He spared a glance from the road to look at his wrist watch. 'We'll be three silly 'uns, belting along here, if Miss Molly's all safe and sound at home by now.'

'She won't be,' Elsie replied morosely.

*　*　*

'I think you'd better go,' Chief Superintendent Hallam told Garrett. 'I don't like these queer calls, but if this one does give us any sort of a lead to Hester Banning and her gang, we simply can't ignore it. Take Norwood with you.'

'Lyndonthorpe,' Norwood commented when Garrett had sought him out. 'Around twenty-two miles from here. I know the place well.'

Norwood drove. He was familiar with all the cross-country short cuts and they reach Lyndonthorpe in forty minutes. To Garrett it was just any sleepy Yorkshire village on any Saturday morning.

'There's a constabulary house here, Dick,' Norwood said. 'I suppose we'd better get in touch with the local bobby first?'

Garrett nodded, and when Norwood had drawn up before a neat cottage with the official plaque attached to it, Garrett got out and knocked at the door. As he stood waiting, looking around him, he thought that, after all, there were worse jobs than that of a country copper.

A pleasant-faced young woman answered the door. She announced herself as Mrs Cranwell and said her husband was out on his rounds and was there anything she could do?

'We're from Regional Crime Squad,' Garrett explained. 'We got a tip-off this morning that some people we're interested in may be living around here. Have any strangers moved in lately, Mrs Cranwell?'

'Only those at the old rectory,' she replied. 'It's been empty a long time, and these folks are thinking of converting it into a private school, from what they told my husband. Of course, he asked to see what authority they had for moving in like that, and they showed him a paper which satisfied him.'

'Have you seen any of these people?'

'No, but my husband told me there was a woman there who smoked all the time and a tall thinnish man with rabbit teeth.'

'Thanks,' Garrett said. 'We'll go and have a talk to them. Where is this old rectory?'

She gave him directions and they drove along the village street to the iron gate Mrs Branwell had mentioned. The padlock which had forced Molly Bilton to climb the gate was no longer there. Garrett glanced along the tree-shaded, neglected drive.

'We'll leave the car here, Barry, and walk up to the house.'

'Right.' Norwood got out, locked the car. They strode along the drive side by side and came to the stretch of weedy gravel which faced the house. As they did so, the front door opened and a man came out on to the steps. Seeing them, he ran down the steps and hurried towards them. The scowl on his face was definitely unwelcoming.

'Who are you, and what d'you want?'

Garrett looked him over. The sergeant had brushed up on Brenda Sheldon's descriptions that morning before he left H.Q.

'I think your name is Smedley,' he said quietly. 'We are police officers from Deniston and we have reason to believe — '

Smedley jerked round and made a dash for it, along the front of the house and into the shrubbery at the far end. Instinctively, Norwood was setting off in pursuit when Garrett grabbed his shoulder.

'We'll pick him up later. I want to get inside that house.'

But they hadn't reached the front door steps before they were confronted by two people who had come quickly from the hall. Garrett recognized Hester Banning and Chuck Stevens. And the woman was holding a gun, very steadily, trained on them. Chuck was a half-pace behind her and they saw the glint of a knife in his hand.

'I heard what you said to Smedley,' the woman grated. 'So stand still, just where you are. Any rushing tactics and you get it — both of you.'

To prove her threat, she depressed the barrel of her weapon. There was a crack and a bullet spurted gravel in front of the policemen.

'Listen to me,' she went on. 'You've just one chance. When I give you the word, you will walk up these steps, between us. You will go into the hall, where I shall give you further orders.' She moved aside quickly, taking up a position at one side of the steps. Chuck made the same movement to the other side.

Garrett said, 'This is silly. You can't get away with it.'

'I can and I will. There's something else you should know. I have a young woman here — Molly Bilton — under guard. Any nonsense from either of you and she will be killed — immediately. Now, get moving!'

Norwood and Garrett had seen the effects of drugs on their addicts before and it was obvious Hester Banning used her own filthy wares. They had a homicidal maniac here. Garrett nudged his companion and, in unison, they took a step forward.

There came a muted twang from somewhere to their left. Hester Banning shrieked, and dropping her gun, clapped both hands to her face. Garrett and Norwood charged simultaneously. Norwood went for Chuck, who was staring at the woman, and took him round the legs in a flying tackle. The knife spun away. As Garrett grabbed Hester Banning, he glanced over his shoulder. Two girls, with a spare, tough-looking man behind them, were racing to the front door. From the man's hand a catapult dangled. He seemed rather pleased with himself. Garrett grinned, twisting Mrs Banning's arms up behind her back. It looked as if the party was over.

18

Though it was Saturday morning, and Chief Superintendent Bill Hallam was officially off duty, he was sitting in his room at Kingsmead House with Spratt, Garrett, Norwood and Brenda Sheldon in attendance, glad enough to tie up the ends of one important case which wouldn't hang on into the following week. Like Spratt and Brenda, he was closely interested in the story Garrett was telling.

'The catapult expert turned out to be Molly Bilton's head stableman, Jim Makin, sir. He had the weapon, with marbles as ammunition, in his car — he'd taken it from his own lad. He and the girls reached Lyndonthorpe rectory just after we did, but they left Makin's car at the rear drive entrance. Makin picked up the catty and marbles just in case.

They got into the back courtyard and saw Molly Bilton signalling to them from behind her barred window. They gathered she was telling them to watch out, that the situation was dangerous. At that moment Smedley came charging round the side of the house, running from us. Makin and the girls grabbed him, bundled him into an outhouse and locked him in. Then they went round into the shrubbery and saw the position Barry and I were in. Makin exercised his skill just at the moment when it was most needed. It was a wonderful shot, the big glass alley he used took the Banning woman clean in the face.

'We immobilized her and Stevens, Makin went back to keep an eye on Smedley. And then the local bobby, Cranwell, came cycling up. His wife had told him about us and he'd ridden along to see if he could be of any assistance.'

Garrett paused, pointing to the pile of cardboard files on Hallam's desk. 'We found that lot without much trouble. And, as you know we also found Buster Siggins dead when we went up to let Miss Bilton out.'

'Yes,' Hallam said slowly, 'Hester

Banning had organized a really big drug-pushing set-up in these parts. We've not only got the principals but the smaller operators here.' He tapped the files. 'The Divisions have had quite a day, rounding them all up.'

'Including Connor, at that cafe,' Spratt put in. 'Yes, it's a clean job. A pack of vermin eliminated — but at the cost of two lives. And what harm they've already done with their foul work we shall never know.'

'Smedley has talked plenty,' Hallam commented. 'He's the type which does sing, high and loud, if he thinks it will benefit him. Poor Buster Siggins took some time to realize just what the gang he'd joined as muscle-man were up to — they told him they were organizing a series of big steals from which he'd get a huge cut. When he did tumble to the truth, he wanted out — fast. They couldn't afford to let him go and talk, so Stevens put the knife in. And young Arnold Toller got the same treatment, of course. On the Monday night when he attacked Mrs Avery, he went to The

Groove and told Stevens what he had done, demanded some sort of protection from them. In the state he was in, it was clear to them he'd shoot off his mouth, if we fingered him as Mrs Avery's assailant, so he had to be killed and they thought they could frame Brenda for his murder by using her car. Stevens phoned him that night, told him to be waiting for them near his house. So he went to the slaughter.'

'It's clear I was followed, probably by Smedley, from the cafe to Morgan's place, and then tailed home by him,' Brenda said. 'I was a bit dim to be hoaxed by that phone call next morning, supposedly from Dave Morgan, but Dave's boys did a good job, didn't they, sir, spotting Bradley and Noyes, the traitor in Dave's camp, who gave such useful information to the gang, at the Red Lion? Noyes put Stevens up to trapping me in Dave's gym, of course. We can get Canfield, the landlord, for harbouring, I suppose?'

'Which,' Garrett said before Hallam could reply, 'leads to the question of Miss

Bilton and those two girls, sir.'

'Yes,' Hallam returned slowly. 'You know, when you reckon it all up, we've been greatly indebted to various members of the general public in this case . . . As for Elsie Thompson and Jean Hathorn, I've had a word with the Governor of Westwood School on the phone. I've explained how the girls have helped us, I've promised to see they are returned on Monday — a job for you, Brenda. Meanwhile, Miss Bilton is looking after them at her place, being surety for them until we pick them up. As she is doing this officially now, I can't see how any harbouring charge against her would stick. And in my view, those two young rips almost rate a Police Medal each.'

'Which they'd probably throw back at us on the spot,' Spratt grunted, and Brenda moved to protest.

'Oh, I don't think so, sir. Elsie Thompson is basically good recruit material, she hinted to me she'd like to be a member of the Force, too. And who knows? If she settles down and has a change of heart, sir, well, it could happen.'

Spratt's laugh was a bark of sheer disbelief.

'That'll be the day!' he said.

THE END